LET ME LOVE YOU

May our love be eternal

I am romantic, loving, sincere and open.
I love this life. Unfortunately, i'm alone.
Be you to whom I can give all my love.
And I will be completely loyal to you.
Extracted from Julia's diary.

FRANCSICO BRITO

LET ME LOVE YOU

May our love be eternal

> I am romantic, loving, sincere and open.
> I love this life. Unfortunately, I'm alone.
> Be you to whom I can give all my love.
> And I will be completely loyal to you.
>
> Extracted from Julia's diary.

Cover Image © Tatiana

Preparation, layout and review: F.A. Brito

Author's email: franciscodeassis.brito@gmail.com

____

Brito, Francisco

Let me love you - May our love be eternal / Francisco Brito

1st. Ed. - São Paulo: Amazon, 2021.

1. Fiction with adult content - Brazilian romance. I. Francisco Brito, 1947.

2. II. Title

____

CHAPTER 1 - Lonely life

Saturday, October 12, 2019 - national holiday.

Julia leaned on the balcony railing and started looking at that immensity of the horizon. Far away was the Copacabana Sea, the princess of the sea.

It seemed that she was lonelier than on other days. And she wondered:

"What is love? Probably many people ask themselves this question, and few people even have difficulty putting it into words. Most people are even startled by this four-letter word. Many people associate this word with problems or a wound in the heart", murmured to Julia.

"All people are devoted to someone. Many people love those who don't. Whoever wants them, they sent them away. And then the vicious circle is formed - whoever I want doesn't want me, whoever wants me sent me away, as a popular song says.

- "For me, love is the affection for a person, a feeling of deep sympathy, a physical attraction. In addition, he has the sympathy and understanding that must be taken into account in a relationship".

"Today when looking at me in the mirror, I looked bad, with a dark eye. I didn't sleep well at night. It could! I haven't had sex in over a year. To relieve myself, I masturbate instead of having sex with a man in the normal way. So, how not to be sad about this situation. When I try to share it with my friends, they say they are in the same situation".

"Holy shit! Where are the men for marriage in this city? So much so that I want to find a great man to delve into each other's hearts and souls, as if we are trying to drown the loneliness in each other's chest".

"The world has evolved in information technology every day. Industries are preparing to work on electric vehicles. Modern televisions are equipped with touch screens, as well as cell phones, the man has already been to the moon, surgery is already being done at leisure. So why didn't scientists make a device that would indicate that a certain person is interested in dating us"?

"Ah, how I want to fly to a desert island and merge into a tribe, where I should be without clothes and with bare feet. It was going to be funny, me in the middle of those Indians with a medium height, and me with 1.78cm in height, much bigger than the average. I would definitely be constantly being teased, with those little ones calling me a giraffe".

"I don't know if I am sad or happy. An inexplicable sensation fills my heart. I'm feeling like a writer who doesn't know the best way to start his storyline or what words to use to start his narrative. All I know is that I want to meet someone with whom I will spend the rest of my life. In return, I will give him a lot of joy and unconditional support to make sure he is the luckiest man to have a woman like me. He would only have to look after me until the end of time".

"I have a lot of ideas on how I will love my man. My head is about to explode with so many fantasies. To scare off those sexual fantasies, I get up and cross the threshold and turn off the light to stay in the gloom. And then I feel a hand sliding around me when I click the last button. And I let that figure's hand go down to my belly because there is nothing wrong with a woman showing indecent behavior. I feel a chill go through my whole body and I can't control what that figure does to me. Just thinking about what will happen next, I lose my mind and when I realize it, I'm masturbating".

"Do you know what I understood after I masturbated? I

understood that loneliness makes us do things that even God doubts. Only those who have loneliness as a partner know what I am saying. The lonely person devotes all his time to loneliness. We build a whole life around solitude. She lives alone and does not want to leave her shelter because she is afraid of happy people. The burden of anxiety is very heavy pressing on our lungs and heart. And he only feels better when he returns to the refuge of solitude that we built ourselves. And then we feel safe".

"I want to leave this paradise called loneliness. I want to find a man who is my life. But the crucial question is where will I find such a man who is ready to share his love with me. The ideal is that I find the man of my life on my way and we both take each other out of solitude, and make our lives full of happiness and love. Then, yes, I was going to open new horizons with him and share my dreams with him. He just had to trust me and I trusted him".

At that time, her cell phone called and she went to answer it and left her reverie - something of those who live in solitude.

CHAPTER 2 - People are afraid of love

Soon the year 2019 will give way to the year 2020. And, goodbye old year. A suffocating damp heat wave of spring hit that late summer day. That spring Saturday was for many people the hottest night in Rio de Janeiro. Thermometers measured 43 ° C, on Avenida Atlantic, but the thermal sensation was 46 ° C, that early evening. It meant Rio de Janeiro was going to have a hotter summer than usual, just compared to the summer of 2010.

Julia sat at the iron table on the balcony of her apartment and moved the table and chair closer to the edge of the balcony to get closer to the air circulation, hoping that there would be a cool breeze to ease that suffocating heat; and she started drinking tea with toast.

There, on the porch, she felt like there was a cool breeze. Only the sensation, because the heat was uniform, to the point of scaring the sea breeze away. The breeze that passed lightly on the porch was warm air.

Sitting there, on the porch, Julia felt even more alone ... She wanted someone to be with her and hold her hand and hold hands with her, talking and making love plans. It was going to make him feel very happy.

This was her worst birthday. She really needed someone in her life to take her hand and make her soul happy. In return, she would do anything to respond to the love she received from her man. She was a beautiful and hot woman, and she had a big heart, a pure soul and a sculptural body to make the girls who are candidates for miss in Rio de Janeiro envy.

Julia was at a low ebb. It hadn't rained in her garden in months. Who would believe that such a woman would be lonely? Her feelings and her intentions of wanting a man to fall in love were like summer rains - the clouds didn't even form and the wind came and carried the clouds to the ocean.

The men she was attracted to, they didn't want anything seriously, just sex. It was as if she had written on her forehead, "I'm easy, easy, to fuck you." She didn't know what else to do to change that stigma of being seen as an easy woman and finding a man for a serious relationship. She wanted to fall in love with an honest and faithful man, to whom she gave all her love.

Faced with that lack of love, she decided to create her own recipe for love to engage in a happy relationship. Armed with a notepad and pen, she went on to write down her ideas of how to grab a man to get married.

She made her own recipe: she caught the lack of sleep, bag under her eyes, wrinkles, tears and wrung it in a meat grinder. She reserved those ingredients and placed them in a sealed container. But she realized that those ingredients were not going to be useful, so she threw them away in an organic waste container.

She continued to make her list useful for her recipe for grabbing a man to marry. She took the smile and put it away. She took the hugs and mixed it up. Then, she put the kisses to sweeten those ingredients. She took passion and mixed it with sensuality, and kept it in a closed container.

It was time to put everything in a blender and mix until uniformly juicy. The recipe was ready. And the next day, she started the day with that dish for breakfast. And she savored spoon by spoon, and drank sweetened coffee to emphasize the taste of her cheerful morning.

Ready. She was prepared for love. She came to understand that true love is when a man is ready to do everything for her, until he takes a star from the sky and gives it to her. But she was alone, there was no one to share her dreams with her. But she had a high self-esteem. She knew by heart what her desire was.

As it was already night, she turned on the light in the room. And twilight launched romantic thoughts about her. She wanted to be with her man of life - no ordinary thoughts. She relieved herself of the day's fatigue and slept. And she dreamed of moments of desires and fantasies, of loving kisses and hugs.

In the morning when she woke up, she didn't want to think about passion and crazy love. She avoided listening to people and paid attention only to what her heart said. She selected what was good for love and discarded perverted thoughts.

She felt comfortable. And he said to himself, "My goal is to find my love". And she cried to destiny that he would look after her and asked that he not hesitate to open the doors of the happiness of love for her.

Since she had no one to talk to, she talked to herself.

"I will not say that I am the most attractive, most beautiful, hottest and most intelligent woman at any time. I will remain humble as a reliable lady and loyal to my future husband. I want to deserve a good and honest man to share his love".

It struck her as strange, but she remained calm and her thoughts balanced. And she told herself that she didn't want to play with other people's feelings. And she added by saying, that she was going to keep her heart open to receive the new love from her soul mate.

The next morning, she realized that the day was flying like a rocket, as much as she wanted, she couldn't for the time. In her mind she saw the future with her full of tenderness and her heart overflowing with love.

A phrase came to her mind and she stammered: "I warmed the bed and I wait for you. Come sleep with me and love me like I'm the only woman in your world. And kindly give me a hug and put the most beautiful dreams in my hands".

She didn't know whether she was sleeping or awake. The

fact is that she realized that she was being enveloped by the magic of love. And she saw that great love was reserved for her in the near future. And as he laid his head on her soft pillow, he saw in his dreams that an escape love was brought to her, but that made her very happy. She jumped under the blanket and she warmed him with her warm arms and hot kisses. She felt his smiling face at that time. She saw that every morning he started with the taste of her lips. So, she wanted to touch him with soft, gentle kisses and whisper in his ear very hungry for sex.

In the morning when she woke up, she remembered that it was her day off. And she went back to bed and reviewed the dream she had that night. And the more she reviewed that dream the more her hunger for sex increased. She had no choice but to masturbate.

Her mood was great. She lay on the other side and slept. This was a good time to rest and spend the whole day in bed. Instead of sleeping, she started fantasizing about having a man by her side, and he was pulling her close to him and their bodies touching and his hands slid over her thighs, belly, beginning the touches that brought her to the peak of desire. And she felt that in her mind her man possessed his soul.

Julia couldn't go back to sleep. Her libido had stirred her body, her blood boiled in her veins. The way was for her to get up and get under the shower and take a cold shower.

She dressed and asked herself:

- "Do you know what my New Year's wish is? I'm going to tell you a secret. My dream is to find a real man who is with me and always supports me. I believe in miracles. Problem of those who do not believe. I believe, she talked to her guardian angel. - "I don't want to just have fun next year. I want to find a man with a strong spirit. I am single, I manage my career as a gynecologist; and, I'm making my own online store of branded clothes go off".

- "I love to travel and please everyone. I am a motivated, strong and confident woman. I want to achieve much more in life. But I need a pillar, on which I can lean. That pillar will be my man that I will marry. But where is this man that I look for like someone looking for a needle in a haystack, but I can't find it". - She murmured.

Julia watched the weather, there, from the wide balcony of her apartment, at R. Gustavo Sampaio, in Leme. Around late at night she started to twinkle some stars in the sky. Around midnight, the sky was partially starry. And Julia kept counting the stars until she lost count.

- "Millions of people around the world can literally look at the starry sky right now. I just don't know why people keep looking at the starry sky. It must be because the huge dark space receives the reflection of the stars that look more like the light of diamonds scattered in the sky", said Julia, looking lost towards the starry sky.

- "It must be because each person is attracted by the thirst for novelty, the thirst to know the unknown, the desire to be unique. People look at the starry sky, trying to find something new for themselves. I shoot for myself; I look at the starry night sky to understand my thoughts". - She murmured. - "As now, I scan the starry patterns in a very interesting uniformity. This makes my thinking clearer".

The coolness of the night was bleak and weak. But it made Julia feel good while she looked at the stars. She didn't get tired of looking at the twinkling stars in the sky.

- "I am sure that people look at the starry sky to see themselves in the stars, alone and distant. Perhaps, people dream of finding a new star, eager to create a special constellation called love. Ah, who will be my star? I hope it won't be long before I find my star to be the love of my life. I really need a real man in my lonely life," she murmured softly when a star crossed the sky and disappeared into the void of the night.

- "May my dreams of finding a good husband come true," she said, crossing her fingers, when she saw another star move and fall into the void of the sky.

She remembered a game she played with her high school sweetheart, when she was a young lady, at Christmas. The joke started asking the boyfriend if he had been a good boy during that year. She asked if he had received a gift on the eve of Christmas night. If he said "no", she said she had an offer for him. And when he asked, she said: "Children get candy. Boys get sweet girls". And she ordered him to look at her, and asked, "Am I sweet enough for you? And before he answered, did she say, "I'm better than sweet"? "If so, take me to you and kiss me". And they kissed. After the kiss, she said: "I have been waiting for you under the Christmas tree for a long time".

He didn't understand.

That was a healthy joke that time leaves behind. Once people become adults, play changes. And people start to protect themselves more and avoid making double-edged games.

Julia was still playful. But she avoided games that would make the man think she was harassing him. Adults see sex in everything.

"You know, today I'm in such a good mood, with the feeling that it won't be long before I find the person, I've been looking for a long time ... I want to take advantage of the opportunity and say that it is very difficult to find a man to marry in Rio de Janeiro. Every guy I know wants to use me, but I just want love and happiness. Am I worthy of it? I want a man who brings me joy and affection... And, for my part, I am ready to give this man affection, affection and feminine warmth. What more does a man want from a woman? I want someone close to me that I can trust and feel protected", she explained to herself.

Julia stared at a star that sparkled in the distance in the sky.

"What do you have to tell me, lone star? I want to tell you that my heart is beating fast. Certainly, you are used to not having emotions of love. Where are the other stars that don't appear? Today is an excellent night to see what is written in the stars. My heart is more agitated today. Are you guessing that the day is coming to meet someone who will give me love and make me happy? I hope, because living without love makes us lose self-esteem", she talked to the star.

Julia remembered the difficult times that she experienced a love disappointment with a scoundrel man. He gave all the signs that he was no good, but she closed her eyes so as not to see what a bastard he was. She insisted on thinking that he was a real man just because he ate her hot. It was not for lack of warning from friends who tried to open his eyes when they said that the man was no good. She didn't believe it and let herself be involved by that man and put him inside her house. She loved him and did everything for him, yet he was able to destroy all her dreams.

It took her time to recover from the damage done to her heart. Those were difficult times that you don't even like to remember. Unfortunately, the pain of love heals very slowly. And when it heals, it leaves the mark of that wound on the heart.

CHAPTER 3 - *The pains of love pass*

Now that the pains of love have passed, and she wanted to find a new man who would give her a chance to be sincere and courageous who would make her love again. She wanted a man who was kind and never rude. Respect, trust and love are the most important qualities to build a relationship.

Julia wanted to be honest with a man. She missed a male shoulder that could give her happiness and peace of mind. In return, she wanted to give him her love and affection. It was her priority to raise a family with a loving man who wanted to have children with her. He just needed to be a real man who wanted a partner to make his life better. She was ready to test his fate.

It was the fourth cup of cold tea she was drinking. Those cups of coffee helped him gather his spirits to open his heart.

Having vented to herself was great, she feels refreshed and comforted. She feels ready to pull herself together and fight for her love. If it is necessary to take risks and act, she is determined to go hunting for her real man. She wants an adult man who knows how to protect and support a woman and give her real care, and who treats her like a woman.

The age difference didn't matter to her. She needed a good experience. She was ready for a serious relationship to build her own family. She wanted to have a happy family. She wanted to hear the laughter of children in the house that she lived with her husband. It was important that this man could set good examples with good practices for his children to understand what is right and wrong.

Julia felt that God had good plans for her. It was only a

matter of time that she was going to find the right man for her. She wanted to experience new feelings and gain experience in an adult relationship. She was not prejudiced against the man's age; she was more interested in his origin; what mattered was her soul and care that he had with her.

Julia was adept that a good man does not hide feelings from her. She would be more interested in knowing what he does, what his plans are for the future. She would return with the same double currency. If he loved her, she would love him twice.

It was her dream to find a man and fall in love with him. She wanted to sleep and wake up with him in the same bed in the morning ... and prepare breakfast for him to have his first meal of the day before going to work. She was sure that the day her eyes crossed her man's eyes, she would know that he was the right man for her. Fate would give her the signal that he was her soul mate. She will listen to you with pleasure.

As for her, she could define herself as a sweet lady. Behind her seriousness was a tender and loving, naive and feminine soul. And if he gave her his heart, she would know how to care as if his heart was a rare crystal jewel, she will never let his heart fall.

Julia was a kind and feminine woman. And she loved romance. She was the type of woman who loved to do good to her man. She believed in astrology and mysticism. When it was something complex, she first consulted the stars. And depending on the signal, she made the decision to make or enter a relationship. As she believed in the sign of destiny, she believed in love at first sight. Because this happens, the person is pulled with a magnet, the palms of the hands get wet and butterflies start to fly in the stomach. At that time everything is beautiful. You don't think about anything else; you just see the possible qualities of that person. At that time, we are able to create a warm atmosphere in a love nest. The person feels perfectly capable of reconciling life with that of the other person.

At that time the phone rang and woke her out of her reverie. She got up and went to answer the phone. It was the wrong call. She hung up and went to do something to eat. The air conditioning in the room was at 17 ºC to allow her to watch TV.

After frying an egg and eating with bread, she went to bathe. When she got out of the bath, she used the towel just to get the excess moisture out of her hair / and, she didn't want to dry her body. With her body wet, she went into the living room naked. She turned on the television and sprawled on the couch. And he waited for sleep to arrive for her to sleep in her king-size bed, between the satin sheets and silk pillowcases.

In the morning, Julia woke up early and went to make her breakfast so she wouldn't be fasting all morning. She had coffee with toast and went to put on clothes to go out. And he went straight to the room she used from time to time as an office to see her friends who came to her for gynecological consultations.

She stopped in front of that gynecological chair and sat on the chair and played with opening and closing her legs.

"The man I am going to get involved with will bring him here to get me so he can practice oral sex on me in that chair. I think he'll like it, for sure. This chair will give us many opportunities and new pleasures," she said to herself.

Julia walked from side to side, with her hand half closed and her index finger crossed across her mouth, imagining the scene of her opening her legs for her man to have oral sex on her.

"He can explore my body. Just imagine! The way I will be in front of him, my legs will be open. Ah, he will definitely like what he will see, ha, ha, ha ... What will he do? When I'm in that position in front of him, I can even imagine his actions. How much it will excite you. Should I get naked to sit on the chair? Or should I sit in the gynecological chair with only the top of the transparent lingerie"?

"Wow, that excited me just to think about it!"

"I will make a red room out of here to be the room for our adult games and enjoy the best of sex every day. Then, whenever we are at home, we enjoy it. That's what I'm going to add my man to," she murmured to herself. - "A lot of passion and love, that's what he will want."

"Will he want to see me in this chair? What toys will he want to use"?

Julia had been excited just to imagine the benefits that her gynecological chair was going to have.

"I will buy edible panties. What flavor will he choose? I will buy him something to wear as soon as I meet my man".

"I will love to see you eat my panties on top of my chased. Everything will be at his disposal. But I will prefer to be without panties on my body".

Julia was thoughtful.

"Is there any prohibited position in sex. It should not have. If not, I will give my man the best sex of his life"? - Murmured Julia.

Julia had the phone number of an "angel" that she had met at Hospital da Lagoa, a week ago, when she accompanied his mother. He had given her a card for her to call him. This was the time to make a phone call. She was not one to take the first step, but the shortage of men in Rio de Janeiro forces women to take the first step in conquering a man.

She had thought a lot about them, about how they could enjoy each other. Now, he was a man. She was just a woman in need of kisses and sex. God would not think it was a sin for a woman to offer herself to a man. After all, it had been a year since it rained in her garden.

In order not to waste time, she was going to have that

room ready for them to be together. She was thinking about how she was going to surprise that candor angel.

"I think I already have several options and plans for our first night of love," she murmured. - I am ready to promise you that I am in his life long before I was born. If he doesn't believe it, I will still offer my body for him to explore like someone who explores a diamond mine".

Julia bit her index finger lightly and wondered how her man was going to behave in the face of the unusual. I will give him what he deserves. I know he deserves to explore every inch of my body. Of course, there won't be time to discuss what to do together. It was everything and everything, there was not going to be "maybe". He just had to like it. She was not a woman of re-strictions nor did she have in her dictionary "this I do not do", "this I do not like to do", "this I will never do". After all, there are no prohibitions on sex. She had the motto: "I can fulfill all your wishes"; "I want to enjoy you every minute".

Her thoughts about the guy made her wet. He had to go change his panties, because of the moisture between her legs. She was enjoying thinking about what she could do with that guy. She could feel his touch on his body, the way he was going to caress her private parts. She hoped he had the strength to do it the way she wanted to. She could smell his passion and his desire to possess her. She imagined the way he was going to take her hips and kiss her for a long time. She already imagined tak-ing his hand and taking him to bathe together.

Will he want to watch television instead of going to bed? Or is it that the fruit that I like, it gnaws to the core? I hope not. I hope he will let me help him undress and pull me under the shower, turn my back to the wall ... and open my ass bands and wash deliciously inside.

That way, she could make her decisions when the time was right. Since that day she met him, she needed his attention. She was ready to make plans for the future with him.

Julia picked up the phone and dialed the number on the card; and a man answered.

- Hello, Robson, speaking! - Said the voice on the other end of the line.

- Hi, I'm Julia who was calling you two weeks ago, when you went to Hospital da Lagoa to take your mother for consultation.

- The doctor, who looked like an angel, so much that she was beautiful? - He said, not content with the fact that she called.

- I called to invite you to go for a coffee together at a friend's bistro, over there at Lido, at Posto 2. - She said.

- I will be delighted to go with you at any time of the day or night. Inviting a woman like you is an order and I will obey, he said. - Just tell me where I can get you to go together.

- I'm on duty today. I'm at home. You can pick me up at Gustavo Sampaio Street, at Posto 1, in Leme, at 5 pm. Is it good for you? - She wanted to know.

- Yes, of course. - He said, all sane.

CHAPTER 4 - The world
was quarantined

Now everything has changed. She, Robson, this world … Covid-19 has made its own adjustments to our lives. Something has changed in people's lives. Now the choice is ours. How he was going to think we could handle it all. She decided to change. She was sure that she was not making a mistake. He was going to be the man of her life. That day, fate had given her the signal.

She wanted to love and be free to explore that man's body as she pleased. Right to choose. And she had chosen him on the first day that she met him. It had been loved at first sight. Or was it the lust she felt for him? Love or lust, the important thing was that she wanted to develop that relationship and be close to him. Or rather say, stay with him from that day on. And that love was eternal, as long as there was pleasurable sex.

She was not horny. She could burst at any moment and enjoy … All for real. She was taking the final step for that love to happen. The good thing there was reciprocity. She hoped he would understand and take that meeting seriously. She wanted him. She hoped he would commune with her plan to be a part of her life.

Robson arrived on time at Julia's building. She was already waiting at the lobby. He didn't even have to park. And the two went to the bistro that served the best coffee in Rio de Janeiro.

At the end of the conversation, Robson proposed to take a trip in his trailer for the unforgettable weekend. It was probably time to get to know her plans and him to get to know hers. After all, she was an adult girl who had been looking for happiness and love for a long time. Who could understand the reasons why she was still alone, single and needy, if she was a successful as doctor? And if that weren't enough, she had the body to shade any odalisque in fairy tales.

She heard him say with all his letters and intentions, the following invitation that you don't make to a lady on the first date. But he unceremoniously invited her.

- How about leaving everything and traveling in a trailer with me? - He said. - And enjoy each other and watch the sunset and the sunrise. I believe that we are worthy of it.

- Wow! You really surprised me. Have you done this before, she asked?

- No. I received the trailer this week. I bought a van in São Paulo and had a bed, a kitchen, a bathroom with a hot shower, air conditioning. A real traveling hotel, he said.

- The invitation is sui generis. But it is very interesting, she said.

- Believe me, you will feel the full range of emotions. It will be a trip to remember, he said.

- With this pandemic the coronavirus is keeping people before the time comes to die, we must enjoy life as long as we have the opportunity, he said.

- Will you give me two weeks to organize my time at work and get to know you better? She asked.

- Yes, of course, he said.

Julia looked at Robson, as she had not looked at a man in a long time.

- Is this serious? Are you sure of your indecent proposal, or is it a joke to test me? She asked.

"Pack your bags in summer clothes and let's go," he said. - I know how to drive. And I will drive very carefully so as not to put you in danger. The trip will be a tour that will start when we leave the house and will end when we set foot inside the house, back.

- Are you sure of the proposal you're making me? She asked.

- If it's good for you and you want it, we can go to a notary and get married under a stable union contract. It is a marriage like a civil marriage, in terms of security for the couple. Next, we will schedule our wedding in the religious and the civil, he said.

- You are crazy about stone. I've never met anyone that crazy. Because only a madman proposes such a thing to a woman. But I liked your proposal. Give me two weeks to think about your proposal, she said.

- Yes, you will have two weeks to think. In the meantime, I will pack my bags for our trip. And to invite two friends to be our witnesses to sign the stable union contract at the registry, he said.

- I will want to go out with you every night to get to know each other better. Putz! This is what I call a surprise, she said. - To marry by means of a stable union, what is the connotation given to the spouses? Yes, because I will continue with my un-married marital status. I will be what for you? Your life part-ners? It is?

- My proposal was abrupt and unexpected. But I would like to receive a positive response. Tell me yes, and let's start a new life together.

Julia just looked at Robson.

- Two weeks from now it will be the holy week holiday, which will give us the opportunity to spend a long weekend together ... It really is our chance to enjoy it, he said. - On the Friday before Holy Week, we will go to the registry office and get married. Life is short. We must not be afraid to take chances. Everything is in our hands.

- And I will be your holiday gift for Holy Week, right!

Maybe you want me to be wrapped in wrapping paper, wearing only panties and a bow, she said.

- I will love the gift, he said.

She laughed an embarrassed but happy smile. After all, it is not every day that a woman receives a marriage proposal like that.

- I propose to get married, and then, we will enter our trailer and go to Campos do Jordão, an aphrodisiac place, with pine forests and the mountains that surround the city of Campos do Jordão. Serra da Mantiqueira, where all types of birds, butterflies and wild animals are sheltered.

- Shall we camp in the middle of the forest? - She wanted to know.

- No. We will sleep in hotels in the city of Campos do Jordão. During the day we will have picnics in safe camps that offer security, where we will not be disturbed, he said.

- It seems like a good plan to meet. This will help us get closer and get to know each other better, said Julia. - But I still find a rush that doesn't suit me.

That attitude by Robson scared Julia. She wanted something lighter, without running over. But what he did was put the cart before the horse. That kind of attitude didn't go with her. She wanted a less anxious boyfriend, not that kind of man. Her intuition told her to get out of that guy, while there was time. It was better for her to wait a little longer and find a real man who would best suit her.

Julia blocked Robson on her cell phone. Afraid that he would come after her, she took a vacation and traveled to the family farm in Petropolis. And she stayed there for two weeks; and from there, she went to Cabo Frio, where she had an apartment.

Julia had some things that she doubted. And one of her secret wishes was to be tied to the bed with a rope so she could feel she was in her man's power. That was what she needed, here and now. She wanted a different emotion. The idea of her being tied to the gynecological chair and being possessed by her man does not leave her mind, to know how much time her feminine energy would be wasted.

She wanted a lot of passion in a relationship to really date, be together on the weekends, travel together and sleep together. She missed a normal man, not a madman like Robson. There are each that the woman has to go through, that even God doubts that there are men like Robson. She only had to look him in the eye to understand that the chemistry between them was not going to happen. She wanted a man who was less quick and less eager to find happiness.

Julia had in mind that to get involved with a man, she would have to spend time just planning the wedding. The "stable union", she would never do that. For her, "stable union" was a way of lying to herself that she was married. It was better to open wide that she was a lover. He didn't roll with her. Getting married would have to be religious and civil, and she would have the status of "married".

She was a mature woman and was ready to prove that she was a woman to marry, not to be an official lover under the "stable union" contract. In her conception, a relationship and love are actions, where it is not just about kissing, living together. She was not the type of woman who liked to talk, she was a woman of action.

She wanted to be with a man who was ready for a serious relationship, love, affection, understanding. He must share with her not only the bed, but also the kitchen, walks, going to the cinema. She was a devoted woman, she wants to take her man and go with him in the same direction, even if the whole world is against it.

Of course, she was interested in knowing her man's desires, how he wanted her, what position was his tare ... maybe she will fulfill them to satisfy him sexually, since they have become close, why not? If he wants love and a life together, she was ready. But, that, only after she knows him better, after smiling a lot at each other and testing the chemistry between them.

There were so many words in her heart that a man needed to hear ... She hoped to find a real man who would give her true love. She wanted mutual love. She will do anything if your man loves her. It is very important to have a person in life who will always be their support in life. She dreamed of a happy future with her man.

Her life belongs to her alone. She had decided to change it and fill it with love, passion and sex. It had been a long time since she had looked for a special man who would take her breath away and make her heart beat faster. He will have to be a man with a capital H, who will take care of her and love her. When he appears, she will give him all the warmth of her heart. She will always be his.

It was a fact that loneliness was killing him. She was looking for a hero to save her. She just needed the love of a man to give her touches, caresses and pleasurable sex. Often, she was very explicit. She played openly with the men who approached her. Perhaps, she needed to be more moderate.

More moderate, she would be a nun. She could go to a convent and dress as a novice. In comparison to other women who are looking for a man, she was the most holy. Because the chicks are attacking without ceremony. Like, all or nothing. Women do whatever they can to win a man and make his day happier.

It could! A large number of women are looking for a relationship with a man, while the universe of men is much smaller than the number of women. The whole world suffers from loneliness, leaving people stressed due to the low expectation of getting married one day.

A woman to hold the man with whom she has a relationship. Competition is fierce between women for a man. So, when a woman is lucky to have a relationship with a man, she must make sure that he does not lose interest in her.

Julia was a brilliant, beautiful woman, without silicone breasts, without inflated lips, without a tattoo, without piercings and without facets in her teeth. She only relied on the gifts that God had given her. She was a thin woman, but in great shape and she was proud of her body that was worked out in gyms for years.

She wondered if it was normal for her to live her whole life and never have fallen in love. Not to say that she never fell in love, she had a boyfriend with whom she lost her innocence in her youth. One good thing he taught her: to give pleasure to another person with the mouth while receiving good pleasure and orgasms.

Julia sought more actions than words. As much as she looked for a man to be her life partner, she did not find it. The men who appeared did not know how to set the tone of the conversation to continue with real actions, whether to fulfill wishes or make decent proposals for a woman.

Too bad he died in a car accident when he was going down the road from Petropolis to Rio de Janeiro. The car he drove blew out the front tire and fell over the precipice. He died, but left his teachings on how she could make her man cheer up and make her day happy.

Julia struggled not to be disappointed with people. But every day facts emerged that left her incredulous with love. People used one part to love and the other half to hate. Neighboring her, a family lived in a very beautiful house. And behind the hedge of ornamental plants was a large glass greenhouse. The interior of the house was illuminated by LED lamps and there were colors that gave the feeling that happiness lived there. She told herself that there must be a real oasis there. It gave him a good feeling of joy. And whenever she passed there, at night, seeing that mansion lit up, she was sure that people were happy there. The owners of that mansion must have had a lot of money and could pay for anything they wanted to buy.

But on that Friday, when she came back from work, as she passed in front of that place, looking all around again, receiving hormones of joy at seeing such a beautiful and harmonious place, she heard a man shout at a woman, which she deduced. be his wife. They shouted and swore, hating each other and wishing each other's death, in complete marital disharmony.

That made her whole world seem to collapse, because she imagined that those who have a lot of money could have happiness and joy. After that, she realized money and material status did not exempt people from hatred and divorce.

From that moment, Julia deduced that it was not enough to have money and live in a luxurious mansion, if there is no love between the couple. What was the point of living in a beautiful house and having a lot of money, if there was no love between the man and the woman who lived inside that house? Days later, she learned that he had left his wife and moved in with a younger woman.

Julia was disappointed with that story. A fifteen-year marriage ends like that. She put herself in that woman's shoes, even though she never saw her. It was those stories that brought her down, causing her to be discredited in the men of the 21st century.

The impression she had was that men only want women only to spend time, not a relationship for life. She did not want to have a wedding with a fixed time to end, as they were with her friends. Of the six co-workers who got married, their husbands left them before they were six years old. This was too frustrating for her.

CHAPTER 5 - Loneliness
makes people sad

At 33 years old, Julia was still single. Solitude made her unhappy. Even so, she made plans for the future. Her intuition told her that the situation was short-lived. Soon she was going to find her love of life. She wanted a strong feeling in her life. She hoped that love was not one-sided, but a pleasant and comfortable relationship that could lead to something more serious and beautiful in the future.

Shining with intimate feelings, Julia tried to find her man of life. She knew that love is not just something that we feel, it is something that a person does. In love she wanted a man who shared her views on life, who was sincere and was not afraid to show emotions. He must be a man who knows how to treat a woman with respect and loving gestures, because a true relationship is one of the most important things in this world between two people.

That morning on Wednesday, November 7, Julia received an invitation to go to the party promoted by socialite Marien Durval.

When opening the invitation, she was surprised by the content of the invitation, which said: "Are you single and lonely? You must be tired of this life without a partner and without love. Let's take care of that, finding the right man for you to get married".

Julia read the invitation and murmured to herself:

- "Party for couples. This will only give you ass, read, read, kiss, stick," she said to herself, after reading the content of the invitation. - "Damn it! And the woman will have to pay the trifle of 5,000 reais to participate in the party. This is what I call equal rights. You want a boyfriend, then pay."

Julia was dying to know if anyone had heard of this party. He picked up the phone and started to call some friends, asking if any of them had heard about this party for couples, promoted by the socialite Mariem Durval.

To his surprise, all his friends knew of the fame of the socialite Mariem Durval, as the socialite "matchmaker". They wanted to know how they could get the invitation, that they would be willing to pay whatever it was for the invitation to participate in Mariem Durval's couple's party. Lucia Helena offered 10,000 reais for Julia's invitation.

After talking to five of her friends from Rio de Janeiro, Julia decided to make the deposit to have the right to go to such a couple's party.

After she left the bank, she murmured, saying:

- "I threw 5,000 reais in the trash can. But I can't resist a curiosity. I will go to such a party. If I get a man to date, I'll be lucky, then it would have been worth it to have paid 5,000 reais. But nothing will get me out of my mind that this is the trickery of this woman who is organizing such a couple's party", she murmured.

- "How people are prone to being deceived, deceived ... Imagine! People pay to go to a couple's party, with no guarantee of getting a boyfriend or their money back. What if the person is not lucky that the saint hits the dance partner's saint? Each goes to his side, without the right to get the money back. Me, huh! But I will be inside. I will go to such a couples party", she said, full of curiosity.

The party was only for single women, or divorced, childless, and unimpeded were invited; and single or divorced men, over 35 years of age and without children were invited. The party organization researched the life of the person to be invited before the invitation was sent. Any taint that the person had at the women's police station or at the civil police station, the person was cut off from the guest list of the couple's party.

The invitation specified that the party was for singles who wanted to meet someone for a possible serious relationship; and get married. Who would take the first step that night would be the women? Each woman would invite a man to the first round of the dance. Once the dance was over, each one returned to their seats. The next initiative came from men, who invited women to dance. It was like that until the definitive pairs were formed. In the end, the event organizer came and asked if anyone wanted to switch pairs.

The party was held in an event house in Gavea. It was a party to meet VIP men and women from Rio de Janeiro, promoted by socialite Marien Durval. She had been doing that kind of event for almost ten years. And from her parties, many couples arrived at the wedding as dreamed of.

It was a real encounter with men who were truly unimpeded and successful in their professional lives. Each guest would pay a trifle of 5,000 reais, with the right to dance dinner, champagne, beer and wine. No distilled drinks were allowed.

Going to that party was meant to meet a man to be her date. Maybe he would be yours for life or for a weekend or two. But she hoped that the man she was paired with at that couple party would become a serious relationship.

His thoughts flew in all directions, as if he wanted to erase the memories of the past. Maybe he was worried about the opportunities she might have or was afraid to make those dreams come true that they were halfway through.

Julia wanted to feel the embrace of a man, to kiss, to hear him say: "I want to love you". Now, more than ever she wants to feel emotions that can be offered by her future boyfriend. Her intuition said that she was going against her great love. She felt more romantic than ever.

Every day she saw dozens of patients and passed by other people and did not realize that she missed the most important thing, the opportunity to be happy. She wasn't going to wait for a miracle anymore. With confidence, she was going to that couple's party. She was a 33-year-old single woman who needed a serious relationship. Her throbbing heart told her that she just needed a man to become part of her life.

Julia dreamed of a man she fell in love with and their bodies merged in a single hug from the night. Her touch burned him with the fire of passion. She wanted to belong to a man, she wanted to give unforgettable nights, she wanted to take care of her man, to give him affection, joy and love. And she would fulfill all his wishes in bed. She would be the way he wanted her to go to him in bed.

Julia did not want a man to see her beautiful and hot just outside, because she had that slim body with great shapes: thin waist, big breasts and butt shaped with weight training and exercises located in gyms. But she wanted men to not only see her butt volume, they would see that she had a soul and a heart. She knew that men are most attracted to women with shapely buttocks. Patience! Every man is crazy swept by the ass, who was she to change that in men. So, she would be the center of attention at that couple's party.

Julia had reached a stage in life that was only interested in men over 40 years of age, because they were more tender. She had in mind that only love is enough, as long as man shows passion and his emotions. This is because all ages are subject to love. It didn't matter to her how old the man was. He could even have a difference in age from the woman, the important thing was if he was ready for a warm and sincere relationship with her.

Julia believed that the woman when marrying a man older than she was a feminine wisdom. Because if a woman chooses an older man it means that she is ready to take care of the family home.

She used to not want to believe in love at first sight because she thought it was just nonsense, but she started to think differently. Love at first is a mutual thing, on both sides. It is never just on one side. She expected something similar to happen at the couple's party. She wanted to feel physically close to a man, to feel his kisses and his hands holding her by the waist while dancing. All she needed was to have a man who loved her and his heart was with her forever. And her heart was hers. She wanted him to feel her and get excited with her hot body, not only at the beginning of their relationship, but always. Because she wanted to be one man and he became her own.

And if it were to have a relationship, it was a real relationship; and just real love and real love. At her age, she understood very well what a real family is. In her view, a relationship must have an objective: to build a family. And family is the work of two loving hearts to make each other happy every day and every night. She was ready to take her man's hand and hold it forever every day, good and bad that life would bring for the couple. She was not the type of woman to run away and say that "love is gone" after the first difficulties, some fights or health problems. If she says "I love you", it is because she really is in love.

Julia was categorical in saying that she believed that true sincere love could only happen if two people fall in love and love each other for what they are. She did not hide from anyone that she was looking for a man to be her lover, life partner, husband who would allow her to feel loved. She was looking for a man to start a family. But for that, she would have to be interested in him, otherwise she wouldn't give herself a chance to start a relationship.

- "This socialite is right to make women the "hunter "of men. It was known that modern men lost the feeling of winning a woman's heart as men did in the past. Men and women have changed roles, now the modern man wants to be won over by a woman".

"I never met a man who took the first step. If the woman doesn't take the first step, the man stays there in his corner, curled up like a snail. Yeah, times have changed", murmured Julia in an audible voice. - Like any woman, I would like to see what it is like when a man tries to win my heart. I must have been born in the wrong generation. Now I am the one who must give the signal, take the first step in conquering man and do everything to please him, if I don't want to lose him to the competition".

- "Well, enough complaining about men. We women need them to be happy with the orgasms they provide us. This couples party will fit like a glove. I will take all my charms to tie a man to make him marry me", she murmured.

"Well, what will not be missing from this party will be beautiful women with silicones on their breasts, botox on their lips and a merchant spirit in their hearts. I hope that the men who go to this party want something real, real fire in the feeling and want to find their soul mate, not a false smile. I'm really tired of being alone. I urgently need a wise and mature man to date and marry".

Her life, as a doctor, had become a living wheel. She didn't have time to have fun. Her life was work, home and work. With the arrival of the pandemic, hospitals were always full of people being hospitalized. The beds were insufficient for so many people infected with covid-19. She took care of herself, but she had to count on luck not to be infected by the virus, brought into the hospital.

- "Men look at me and want me. When I go for walk-in sports clothes, I notice that men are bent over and stumble to look at and admire my ass. I must understand the value of male opinions. They are men who dream of satisfying their libido, she murmured to herself. - "I know they won't look at my soul, they won't share my hobbies or the way I think, they are only concerned with satisfying their libido. But I like to feel how men look at me. It is a hope that men will be hunters again, instead of being hunted".

- "Yesterday I came across a humorous program in which a comedian said that the best gift from a woman to a man is that she does not interfere with the things he is doing. And he added, saying that the man expects from his wife that when he is watching TV, the woman will make him a sandwich and take him to eat, drinking a cold beer, and let him enjoy the program he chose, especially if it is his team that playing. Amaze! The audience applauded him, frantically. I thought that was absurd. So, the man prefers to stay on the couch watching TV, drinking beer, instead of talking to his wife? The world really is upside down". - She raged.

- "Say what you say, but the destiny is above us and can help us women to get rid of men like that. Instead, fate leads us to a good, kind, faithful, hardworking man who helps the woman make dinner, helps make breakfast with scrambled eggs and bacon, or go to the street to buy bread while we make coffee in the morning. Because only with the help from above will he be able to save his wife from mediocre men and profiteers". - Said Julia, disbelieving men.

Julia was almost convinced that marriage is a restriction on women's freedom. But another side of her told her that marriage is being with the loved one who supports you, who becomes her joy and pleasure. His guardian angel whispered in his ear that a loving couple can divide adversity in two and double happiness. Then her soul told her: that marriage has many advantages, such as sharing different moments, like reading together in bed before going to sleep, making love at dawn, snuggling together with your nose in your neck. As a woman, she understood that she could live without marriage, but it would be much better if she was lucky to ever get married.

Julia was excited to go to the "couples party". She hoped to find a boyfriend at that party. After all, she had paid 5,000 reais to go to that party to find a boyfriend. She was already tired of that life of work, home and work. She wanted more than to have that life more or less. She woke up every day at the same time and did the same things.

She dreamed of belonging to a man who would always love her. What could be better than a romantic kiss, sex and breakfast to start a new day? One thing she was sure of, she wasn't going to hide her true emotions from the man who met him at that party.

Now, if you want power, she wanted a sincere, honest and serious relationship. She was optimistic about going to that party that Saturday. Who knows what fish would fall in her net! She deserved to be happy.

CHAPTER 6 - People should love like animals

Friday, November 29, 2019. Soon Julia got up and went on her usual walk on the Copacabana Boardwalk - South Zone of Rio de Janeiro.

As she walked, Julia remembered the questions she was asked when she was a girl and entered adolescence: "what will you want to be when you grow up"?

She dreamed of being an actress, wife and millionaire, when she was a young woman. But, none of her dreams were realized. She was 33 years old and still single. By imposition of her mother who was a doctor, she managed to graduate in medicine and today was a gynecologist.

Now, she dreamed only of loving and being loved by a real, straight and sincere man. She hoped to find a man who was not in need of other men's jealousy or wanted to change the way he was.

What she was able to enjoy from her dreams as a girl was that she grew up and her dreams changed throughout her life. Dreams grew with her. She continues to believe that her dream of getting married will come true. She just doesn't know when it will happen. She now dreamed of marrying an honest, sincere and faithful man, who would grow old with him beside her, without the need for jealousy of other women or business trips that would leave her alone at home.

She needs the help of that "Guy from up there" and destiny, who are the future owners of her. Life will continue to change everything in her own way, including her childhood dreams that have been changing year by year, taking on new forms. But they did not stop growing with it. Dreams never end.

Julia was romantic and sentimental by nature. She was sure it wasn't just people who had the prerogative to love, animals could love themselves like people. The greatest example of love among animals that Julia has ever witnessed was when her puppy Sissi, a Scottish Fox Terrier breed, went into labor and she took Sissi to her friend's veterinary clinic, since Sissi was suffering a lot from the birth pains.

It wasn't long before Julia's mother arrived, bringing Sissi's husband, Sauer. He whimpered at the reception that the vet decided to let him into the operating room, where Sissi was in labor.

The veterinarian put Sauer on the table next to Sissi. The Sissi immediately calmed down when she felt Sauer's presence on either side. He stroked her paw when she grunted in pain, and she calmed down. He was affectionate to her throughout the labor. And she was able to safely give birth to three puppies: two females and a male. It seemed to Julia that there was real love between those two animals. It proved that in this world even animals find their soul mates.

- "All beings have their soul mates. Everyone finds their own somewhere, murmured Julia. - And where will my soulmate who does not appear, no matter how much I have searched".

She needed love, passion, trust, because she was a woman, she has feelings for a true love relationship. She was aware that a relationship was not just kisses and sex, the woman has to work on it and improve herself for the sake of the person with whom she wants to live a great love. She was sure that if she met a real man that night, her true self would be revealed to her. She was ready for a harmonious relationship with a mature man; and get married.

Her thinking was twofold: one believed in soul mates; and the other believed that true love existed. One thing she was sure of: love is the only thing worth wanting.

She swore that when she found her love, she would strive to learn how to make her delivery better. She was going to be more loving, using her mind and heart. Anyone who has ever known love closely knows that love is difficult to predict the next moment.

Some people believe in destiny, others believe in a special power, others believe our lives are written before we are born; and there are those who believe in God because love emanates from God. Therefore, it is God who sends a special person to be someone's partner. She would like to meet someone who brought the gift, laughs at her heart and is not afraid to love and be loved.

She does not think that life was made of illusion, but of moments. Today we share our emotions with someone, tomorrow we don't want to see that person painted blue or black. This is because that person who appeared in our life and then disappeared was not yet the person with the wisdom to teach us to love and fill us with passion and love.

- "It is so nice to meet a person with whom we identify. And that person becomes a ray of sunshine that helps us to keep the clouds away. I haven't had fun with someone in the moonlight for a long time". - Julia thought aloud. - "For me, the family is above everything. That's why I want to create a stable relationship with a man".

Julia was the type of woman who always had warm hands and some parts of her body were a living oven. As a doctor, she was willing to teach her future boyfriend a lesson about the woman's body structure and the three levels of pleasure. This is because some men, even those with years of experience, many do not know what women want.

Not knowing the structure of the woman's body, let alone

what she thinks, the man is skating in the dry. As the woman does not give the coordinates of her erogenous areas, the man keeps making many attempts to discover the "G" point. And he ends up giving up and starts to do the basics, and stops trying to discover the woman's erogenous zones.

With good reason, since the parts of the female body are very complex. Especially the private parts - such erogenous zones. For some women it can be the belly, the neck or the ears. For other women, her entire body is a solid erogenous zone that a man must explore with his lips and tongue. Like mistakes and hits.

But if the woman helps the man to find the secret places on her body, she will have a good lover. The man will soon learn which points to touch, since the woman's erogenous zones is a mathematical axiom that not every man will have the chance to know or know how to explore. This is why he has so many women that he says he never had an orgasm.

Every man should be a pioneer of the woman's body. It will be a lot of fun and interesting to try to discover the woman's erogenous zones to build the bridge that will lead you to discover what gives you the most pleasure. Few men worry about fetishes in the intimacy of the couple. Often, the man is afraid to discuss this with his girlfriend, wife or lover, and issues that could be discussed are left over for later, and are never discussed or resolved.

The world has about 7.8 billion people, of which there are about 4 billion men in the world. So why are there so many single women, alone and lonely? Perhaps, because many men are not ready for a relationship, then they wait for only the woman to do everything for them.

The woman, in turn, wants a man who proves to be a real man and who does everything she wants him to do. And as the man does not guess, she cannot achieve what she expects so much of him.

But many men have the souls of a king and want to have a harem of beautiful women to lead them to the fairytale castle. He thinks that because he has an erection, it is enough for a woman to spread her legs for him to penetrate. She wants to get his "timer" to come, otherwise he comes first, then goodbye what was nice for her. It was certainly not the kind of man she wanted to find to marry.

Julia knew that in order to attract a partner, people should smile with joy, showing happiness, because no one likes serious or moody people. Laughter is a necessary emotion for communication between people. It doesn't matter if we are human beings, rats, dogs or chimpanzees, because it is the smile that attracts interlocutors, partners and people with similar ideas.

It is crucial that people smile more among people. Or even in text messages, people try to transmit their laughter with the help of emotions, the so-called "rs" or brackets)))). There is no lack of smiles to win the person you love.

Julia had refined tastes and other staggering ones. She was crazy about coffee with milk with caramel sauce and fruit tea - An interesting combination, the same as her. She loved diversity in everything, whether in clothes or food, depending on the mood she was in.

That morning, she had dawned with a sporting spirit. In those days, she wouldn't wear high heels or an elegant dress, she would wear jeans and loafers. Her soul seethed with incessant passions of love that she wanted to channel to a loved one. She was more smiling than on other days.

Soon she went to Copacabana beach and sat on the sand, close to breaking the tide, and watched the waves for a long time. It was relaxing and fascinating. Even though she was a pragmatic woman, her heart really wanted feminine happiness and a family with a man. From her soulmate, she dreamed of obtaining tenderness, love and loving stability.

That day, she had a lonely heart and wanted love and sex.

Who could give her the love she needed? She was going to respect the man she came to marry. She was looking forward to the day of the socialite Marien Durval's wedding party.

She was hoping to find a man who would make her breathe full of passion. She was a predator in the overwhelming expectation of the desired. She imagined the touches of warm lips in a sweet kiss and the touch of gentle hands that would hug her gently, lighting the fire all over her body.

Julia was a resilient woman with a good female figure. But she was tired of being alone. She had everything she needed for life, but the fact that he didn't have a man who loved her left her feeling worthless. It could! It had been a long time since she had felt the emotions of being in love with a man who loved her, respected her, was faithful and dedicated to her. That was all she needed to be happy. The fact that the man was older than she didn't matter. The most important thing was love and feelings.

She did not understand the reasons for not finding a man to marry, if she was not arrogant nor looked like a Barbie doll, she had no plastic surgery and her lips did not look like a monkey's ass. She was all natural, feminine and her body was young and tender. Nor were there any special mysteries in it that would drive men away from her. She did not understand why men were afraid of her. She had only one explanation for this: she was too hot and a doctor.

Julia had so much accumulated energy that she wanted to share it with a man who would make her explode with passion and desire. It could! She radiated sexual energy that let men see her with malicious thoughts. One thing she was sure of, she was ready to dive with a man into the world of love and passion.

Julia wanted a man in her life who was not afraid to show his feelings for her. In return, she would give him all her love, tenderness and attention. Together she would strive to build a healthy relationship with him to be together in the present and the future. She was one of those women who wants everything or everything with her man. Her only phobia was to be abandoned by the man she married.

She was a very versatile woman, in the sense that she was not only developed in different areas of life, but was still very balanced in life, reasonable, as an insanely passionate woman who knew how to give and receive love. No, of course she was not perfect, but you could safely call her a balanced woman.

She was just a beautiful, hot woman with a million dreams. She just needed a man to be happy. She wanted to give him everything he needed and wanted from her.

Julia considered that love happens accidentally, in the blink of an eye, in a single pulsating and intermittent moment, love can arise and everything happen, and the me and you exist. She was aware that there are no ideal people, because all beings have their secrets, but she would like to find that man she would trust and say whatever he wants. Her heart was open to passion, love and sex, in that order.

She believed in destiny. There was a great love that screamed inside her, which is why she was going to keep looking for the man in her life to own her body and love. After all, she was a serious marriage-oriented woman. She wanted only one man for her life. She didn't want to remain that strong woman, owner of her destiny. She wanted to find a man who was honest and loyal to her who would help her achieve her goals: getting married, having children and being happier. That was why she wanted to gift her special feelings only to a man who was ready to win her heart and become a part of her life.

She wanted to share everything with her future husband - shared joy and double joy. That was the only way she knew how to give her loved one the chance to love each other enough to make the relationship last.

Julia needed a man because it is more pleasant for two to enjoy the joys of life than for one. Together, joy multiplies and sadness splits in two. Mathematically, as a result, there is twice as little sadness; and there is twice as much joy. She wanted a man with whom she will feel good and happy with him; and with whom she will make love.

CHAPTER 7 – Sexuality in
the 21st century

That morning, Julia had a talk in the hospital auditorium about "sexuality in the 21st century". It was a passionate subject, but it was also very contradictory. It was a topic she didn't like to talk about in her lectures, but event organizers always asked her to talk about that topic. Perhaps, because she is a Gynecological Doctor. But talking about homosexuality was too complex, even though she had already participated in a study group on sexual orientation in the 21st century. However, the studies she had participated in did not reach any satisfactory results, as there were multiple interpretations about the theme "homosexuality".

In her lectures on sexuality and homosexuality, Julia spoke of the sexual moment in Brazil, but avoided delving into the core of the negative issues that it was the man or woman publicly assuming their sexual option - men who are attractive and have sex with men; and women who are attractive and have sex with other women.

When someone asked her if the 21st century was a century of gene mutation, which is why so many boys and girls were born who turned out to be homosexuals over time, she said she was unaware of any study that proved any theory that people (man and woman) were born with a propensity to be gay.

Others asked if it was a sign of the end of the world to have so many homosexuals - gays and lesbians. She replied that she could not answer such a question, since there was no scientific evidence. And she was trying to get off on a tangent.

When she had no way out, she replied that despite several studies carried out on homosexuality, no study had reached any conclusion as to whether or not there was any genetic basis for so many gay men and so many lesbian women. To ease people's questions about homosexuality, she said that the world was witnessing a large number of people who are declaring themselves to be gay. But she couldn't say whether children with more genes of a gender were being born, resulting in so many gays, lesbians, bisexuals, transsexuals and transgenders.

When the questions were many, she said that the growing number of men and women was undeniable that with the passage of time of existence and sexual experience between men and women, they discovered that their greatest attraction was for people of the same sex.

In daily life, she had witnessed many married women who after years of marriage and with children, they leave their husbands and children to go and live with another woman. The same was true of well-married men and children, who after years of living together, one day discover that they are having greater attractiveness for another man, and they left their family to go and live with other men.

However, no study had shown results on any substance used in water or pest control in crops, or that the microwave device was emitting any substance that would alter people's genes. She was unaware of any study that revealed what caused changes in gene variation during the development of the fetus in the mother's womb.

Julia stressed that it could be possible that there was some substance in the food or water that one drinks that was causing alteration and variation in testosterone in boys and girls, interfering in the sexual orientation of boys and girls when they grew up, since there was a large number of girls who, when they grew up, began to feel greater attraction for girls; and boys who, when they were young, started to feel more attractive to boys.

In her lectures, Julia was blunt in saying that she still did not have a scientific study that proved that the partial feminization of some boys and the partial masculinization of some girls were related to the food or water that the mother had consumed during the gestation.

As no study had proven what led to the phenomenon of homosexuality in people in the 21st century. It could only say that the world was becoming different segments of sexuality. But all that was said about gays and lesbians was pure speculation. It was the same as speculating who was born first, the chicken or the egg.

For a while, Julia participated in a group of studies on the births of children who were born with male organs and girls who were born with female organs, but over time they chose to have relationships with people of the same sex. But she had stopped participating in the group because she did not see satisfactory results. She preferred to abstain from that research, leaving that group of researchers on the phenomenon of homosexuality for good.

Many of Julia's colleagues, with whom she had graduated in medicine from university, dated, engaged and married, had children, but after a few years of marriage they left their husbands and went to live a great love with another woman. And the same had happened with some of his friends who were born, grew up, became adults and got married, started a family, but that one day he was enchanted by another man and left his wife and children to go and live a great love with another man.

As a gynecologist, she argued that there is a very high tendency for men and women to become bisexual; and other married people divorced to embrace their new sexual option, coming out of the closet and assumed they were gay.

She argued that the world since the world is a world has shown itself to reveal the sexual tendencies of humanity. The fact is that nobody knows where the new generation of the 21st century is going. The fact is that homosexuality is a reality in modern society. It is no longer said that homosexuality is a disease or the result of some sin that the parents committed and as a punishment they had gay sons or lesbian daughters.

Today society has created laws to protect homosexuals. Even laws were created to legalize marriage between equals, that is, between people of the same sex, in all social classes. Julia herself had a lesbian sister and some cousins who were gay, but they were no less important than she was. To end that matter, Julia said that there was no heterosexual woman, but a woman. And she said she was sure that until that day, she had not been attracted to another woman, but she did not say that of that fruit she would never eat.

She exalted that until that time she had only had sexual affinity for the opposite sex. And she concluded by saying that only time will tell when she would be a woman with attractiveness for the opposite sex. And she stressed that everything changes, even people's genes. And to finish her lecture, she quoted a song, in which the author says that "nothing that was will be the way it was a second ago".

After Julia left that lecture, she went to dinner at her parents' house. And she took the opportunity to sleep in her old bed. It was in conversations with her mother and father that she recycled herself about the present and the future.

CHAPTER 8 - The party for couples

Friday, December 6, Julia went to the couples' party that took place twice a year, at the socialite Mariem Durval's house, known as the "Matchmaking Lady".

Julia was anxious to know what was going on at the couples' party promoted by this socialite. She had no idea what she was going to find at such a couple's party she had been invited to.

She really didn't know how that socialite had found her address. Maybe because she is a gynecologist and works like crazy in a hospital in the South Zone of Rio. Someone she has seen, and that person has indicated her to that matchmaking socialite.

Okay, she was a dignified, charming, attractive, sincere and romantic woman with a good character. But nobody has a crystal ball to guess that this or that person is suitable to be invited to a party in Rio's high society. Someone must have seen her in one of the clinics delivering a baby and liked the way she was a queen who knew how to give affection, tenderness and passion to a lonely man.

Julia saw love as a fire, once lit, it doesn't take long and will soon burst into flames. She was grateful to the person who nominated her for that socialite to include her name on the list of VIP guests for that "couples party", promoted by socialite Mariem Durval.

After all, life requires that human beings live in pairs - man with woman. But what was seen most in modern society today were men with men; and women with women.

It was 15 minutes to 22:00, when Julia accessed the parking lot of the luxurious party house, in the sophisticated Gavea neighborhood, on R. Mary Pessoa. She handed the key to the valet to park her car. And she was taken by a girl to the waiting room. Who came to assist her was the socialite Mariem Durval, in person, smiling and talking.

While Julia was taken to another living room, in a sophisticated environment, she let her thoughts fly in all directions of that elegant place of great taste.

- "Sometimes life wants to take us in a straight line, but destiny makes us spin in a zigzag that makes us dizzy. That is where we fall into a spill like that; and we have difficulty getting up", she thought, afraid of what she would find there.

Julia always had the courage to express everything she felt and face all difficult situations. She was unmoved by little, but that environment bothered her. That was to leave people with their mouths open, so much so that the atmosphere is glamorous.

Her thoughts scared her, but she was already there and she had to find the courage where she didn't have to fight for her purposes: to find a man to marry.

"It is a sign of the new times, it can only. The woman pays to go to a party to find a boyfriend! At least if I find a serious, trustworthy and educated man here today who knows how to make his wife happy, it was worth the invitation," she murmured to herself.

From her life experience, she knew two basic things: she always has to take chances; and the consequences of taking risks must be taken. She was raised to get married and be happy. Okay, life isn't always as bright as we want.

"And here I am at a "Couple´s party" to find a man to be my boyfriend. Well, since I debuted in the rain, I can't be afraid of getting wet, murmured Julia. - I hope he is a real man and knows that the hole is further down".

Julia was not one of those women who keeps wondering how many shoes a woman needs to have total happiness. She was practical, sweet, energetic and very sociable. And on top of that she was of a romantic nature, she is able to make wishes to a star that changes places and to walk all night in the moonlight. She was able to get in the car and go watch the sunset in the late afternoon with the man she is in love with.

At that time the girls began to arrive for the "Couple´s party", brought by Mariem's hand, one by one, and introduced the girls who were already waiting for the party to begin. They talked friendly, as if they had known each other for years, such was the harmony that they had with each other. And then the other women arrived for the party.

After the last girl arrived, Mariem took them to the great dance hall. At that time the men were brought in to brighten the party. They were introduced to the women, one by one, who had shining eyes, each more sympathetic than the other. After the introductions, they were taken to the dining room. And everyone sat at the tables, all mixed up. No table remained man to man or woman to woman.

They talked the trivial. Julia remembered a phrase that she had read somewhere, that, as a rule, you should never ask a woman a question when she is hungry. And by the way, all those girls were hungry. That rule seemed convincing, because when women are hungry, their mood is not very good, so it is very likely to be more negative. Certainly, the party organizer should have known about that rule. For this reason, Mariem Durval took the girls and men to settle down to be served dinner.

Julia had never been aware of that detail. That night the plug came on and she understood that strategy of men inviting women they are interested in to take them out to dinner. It is because they understood that to get a positive response from the woman, they invited them to dinner for something delicious to satisfy their hunger. And, of course, they did not forget dessert, with sweets of different flavors, a way to make women relax. They knew that after dinner and dessert, their chances of getting a positive response from the woman would be much greater.

As Julia was hungry, she ate to quench her stomach. With hunger satisfied, she would listen more carefully to the proposal of her would-be future boyfriend that night. And night promised. Her heart was open and full of love. She couldn't forget that time runs at full speed, without paying attention to people's pleas. And there is no way to stop its speed.

Julia had in her favor the beauty of her body with its large shapes. And the men had already noticed her shapes, she had already noticed by the look of each one of them. She would have to be meticulous to take advantage of that moment and choose the man who least looked like a scoundrel and seemed most worthy of her heart.

As the woman had been given the choice to invite the first man to dance, she chose Silverio Tomaz Ribeiro, a CEO of a construction company in Rio de Janeiro. It was love at first sight and their bodies gave themselves as mouth to ice cream. They did not detach themselves all night as if their souls had been well mixed like coffee with milk.

There was empathy and joy between the two, passions being channeled on both sides, causing surrender based on the similarity of points of view and thoughts, feelings and needs of love. Each was delighted with the pleasure of having each other. They were not just a couple who loved each other at first sight, but became best friends. The courtship became true, with the foreshadowing that the romance could last for many years and the couple never split up.

As much as she wanted to go with him to a motel, she stopped herself and did not meet that mind-blowing desire. She wanted that man forever, not for a night of sex. But she couldn't take that hoax of being "a chaste woman" for long. The temptation was greater than her judgment.

After two weeks of dating Silverio, she decided to give it to him. And she promised him that she would prepare the memorable night to welcome him into his life before the wedding, leaving him happy and believing that she would be marrying a woman "chaste who had not yet slept with another man". He would be the first in her life.

Julia, as much as she wanted to take Silverio to sleep with her, preferred to hold the "precheca" (vagina) and not go and spread her legs for him. First, she was going to meet him, while playing a good girl, chaste and pure.

She thought about him all the time. For him, she would climb the mountain to be with him. She would be delighted to sleep with him, but she had to go slowly the saint is made of clay to let the saint fall. As much as she thought he was an extraordinary person, she knew that a man's heart is land that no woman can walk without falling. But she was going to give it to him, because she had chosen him to be her man. She wanted to hold his hand, hug him tightly, kiss him gently and let him rest his head on his chest to hear his heart beat just for her.

It had been a long time since she had been feeling as happy as she was feeling beside him. There was no one she would rather be with than him. She confessed that he was the most intense beginning of her endless love story. He was by far the best man to own his heart and his feelings, his soul, his body and his joy. She felt she belonged to him entirely.

Julia was stepping on the clouds with the love that man gave her in the smallest details. She felt he would do anything for her, until he climbed mountains for her. She wanted to be everything to him, and allowed her heart to want him that way. With him it was her favorite place to stay. Every moment with him was an invaluable treasure.

She could call her crazy, but she couldn't stop thinking

about Silverio. She loved him and wanted to marry him because he was in her, no matter if several walls separated them, she wanted him to be with her in their minds. She wanted to guarantee her presence in his thoughts so that her feelings for each other would never be weakened. And since she was ready to build relationships with him in real life, the best they would do was get married soon.

He occupied her mind all the time, like an addiction. She didn't complain because that was the best feeling for her. She lived a moment of crazy love, in a world of softness and passion. She was ready to be a man for her entire life. She wanted to sleep and wake up next to him every day for the rest of their lives. She knew it wasn't his first love or his first kiss, but she wanted to be his last in everything.

She no longer worked well, so much so that she was distracted by thinking of Silverio. For him, she would face each new day for them to be together. She had it in her heart, beating at the speed of light. Being in love was her best frame of mind. She liked him and wanted to live with him, breathing the same air that he breathed. He was a wonderful man, the man of his dreams. All she did was think about him. There was only twice that she wanted to be with him: now and forever.

The more she thought about him, the more she understood that he was the one she needed in her world. She liked him and had no words to describe that kind of feeling in her heart. She imagined him to be with her wherever she went.

He often tried to find words to describe what he felt for him, but no word or cliché could do it justice. All she wanted was to be with him day and night. She had never thought that one day she would be in a position to try to explain how much a man would mean to her, how she lived now.

All her love was kept in her heart for him. So how could she not want to marry a man like this if her heart was beating for him every second! This was an incredible fact that could not be denied. All that feeling made her want to embrace him from today until the next two hundred years.

She fell in love with him every day because it was his special place in her heart. It all made her freak out, like he was an addiction that made her addicted to love.

She now agreed that people do foolish things for love. She was determined to follow him anywhere and be his. He was her best hello. He was her soulmate, if not how to explain that there are 7.125 billion people in the world and she had chosen that man to love. He was simply her best and greatest love of life. Now, all she wanted to say was that she couldn't live without him. He was the best thing that ever happened to him. She adored him with heart and soul, and wanted him to know that he was her angel. He made her excited, nervous, and crazy about him. Above all, she wanted him to make her happy every start of every day.

Julia missed Silverio so much that she couldn't stand being away from him anymore. She really wanted to be with him and his body to be just for him. She wanted to marry him to sleep together every night and have breakfast together in the morning, being the happiest people in the world.

As much as Julia thought that there was no real man who was her stronghold, she was surprised by her sudden change, since she met Silverio. She realized that the happiness of life is the certainty that we are loved. There were mutual sympathies between them. She had no reason to postpone that night of love with Silverio before she lost him.

Julia could not disappoint that man thirsty for love for her, passionate and full of love to give her. She hired a friend's buffet to serve dinner for her as her special guest that night.

During that week, Julia massaged the vagina with astringent gel and washed with a stone bath to tighten the orifice walls of the vagina. And on "D" day, Julia prepared a dinner to welcome Augusto Silverio to her house.

Julia gave the employee a break for that weekend. After she had taken care of ornamenting the candles in the candlesticks, the flowers in the jars, the maid left, since dinner was going to be served by her cousin's buffet.

That dinner was the key to opening the doors of love. She wanted to give her partner a lot of pleasure. She had realized that love changes people from the inside out. That concern about doing the right things for that dinner made her realize that the man had changed her life. She was changed. She was really in love. This was her chance to grab that man and get married. He had dared to break the ice in his heart and fill the void in his soul. She was going to repay him with a night of unforgettable sex for him. It was her chance to hook that big fish.

Being happy has always been her goal. That man was the key to her happiness. She had chosen him to have a life together. It was with him that she wanted to do crazy things. She wanted to be unique to him; and he is unique to her. She was going to strive to show him that happiness exists when you find the magic of love and happiness. Love takes us to heaven.

After a month of dating, on January 10, 2020, Silverio asked Julia to marry him, giving her a white gold solitaire with 100 diamond points, which had cost just over 66 thousand reais, sealing that one engagement in style.

The following week, they went to the registry office and scheduled the wedding for March 13th. After marking the wedding day, they informed the socialite of their decision to get married in forty days, time to run the proclamations for the civil wedding.

Julia was not happy. She was sure that she had been blessed by God when she chose Silverio at the couple's party; and now that she had agreed to be engaged to that man full of attitude.

The fact that he traveled every week was no reason to give up on that relationship. He was fascinated by Julia's beauty. She saw sincerity in Silverio's promises. She accepted his request, and said yes to his offer. As much as one side of her said it was too early for her to take on that responsibility, and she wasn't going to be cruel and say no to her marriage proposal. After all, he proved to be a gentleman and able to show as much love to her as he was doing.

CHAPTER 9 - The wedding

That Friday, March 13th, the wedding party was at the socialite Mariem Durval's "couples party" house, to celebrate the thirtieth wedding that she had been Cupid. Mariem Durval had invited the thirty couples who married under her blessing as a "matchmaking fairy".

Julia's mother and father were present; and Augusto Silverio's parents. Julia's father came in with the bride; and Augusto Silverio came in with his mother.

Mariem started her ceremony with the following words:

- "Husband and wife should not only be people who love each other, but also best friends. So, like this, the marriage can last for many years and the couple will never be separated", he said to Mariem.

- "None of the marriages that I was cupid was divorced. I reaffirm for each couple that met on the premises of this house of parties of couples and got married here, to create true friendship for each other and never to separate. So, I repeat to you two who are getting married today the following: Get old together. When you are out of patience with each other, take a trip and make peace. Aim when you get married to be able to complete twenty-five years of marriage. There, we will celebrate its silver anniversary, 25 years of union and achievements, and thus renew the vows taken on the wedding day". - Said Mariem Durval, very touched to be having the thirtieth wedding in her house of parties of couples.

- "Nothing under this floor is more important than the union of a man and a woman, in what was called a "marriage". It is from the marriage that the woman procreates happy, knowing that she has a life partner who will help her to take care of the offspring. Therefore, never break the vow that you will do before God, those present and your parents. Divorce was man's worst invention. Therefore, when getting married, the couple must respect and deny the temptation of divorce to have a new husband. Do not be fooled by the new marriage and the new sexual pleasure, because changing men is changing problems. Stay with your man and renew the vows of love every day from the beginning of the relationship. Give each other happiness, care, love and affection and lots of sex. Really build the happy reality of conjugal love". - concluded the ceremonialist, Mariem Durval, who spoke eloquently.

Each has its own life rituals. And fate comes and loads the plans that were made with so many details. The honeymoon trip of the couple Silverio and Julia, in Aruba, was postponed due to the closing of borders and suspension of flights to that country to contain the advance of the covid-19.

There was a time when the world was adopting quarantine measures to contain the coronavirus pandemic. Airports were closed and flights were suspended, and those with a scheduled ticket had to cancel the trip. The Coronavirus pandemic required that different countries take strict measures to contain a higher incidence of the disease in Europe and the rest of the world.

Julia and Silverio were happy to enjoy their honeymoon in Rio das Ostras, at Silverio's parents' beach house. They went by helicopter to Rio das Ostras.

When the first rays of sunlight entered the room, Silverio woke Julia with kisses and touches to light her fire.

- My love again? We spent the whole night fucking. And do you want it again? - She said. - But, since you want, then eat me with pleasure that I am all yours that the function of the honeymoon is to fuck, we are here for that.

- A woman with a sculptural body like hers and the most perfect ass I have ever seen, it is natural that I have addicted to you, and want to fuck you at any time of the day or night, he said. - I am the happiest man in the world to have a woman as hot as you in bed, being all mine.

- You are a perfect husband, my love. Eat me and don't feel sorry for me. Women are happy only when they are well fucked, she said. Make me happy because I am in my best years to fall in love and sexually perfect for love.

Julia tried to prove to Silverio that the average moment of pleasure lasts only eleven minutes. But not everyone is willing to sacrifice everything for these eternal moments. She knew that this world is measured in eleven minutes. Absolutely everything, and people live to get those eleven minutes. And the world spins throughout these eleven minutes. It is because of these eleven minutes that people get married, form families, support crying babies, buy expensive clothes, support a gigantic cosmetics industry, women go on diets and sacrifice themselves by preparing themselves physically for their man, pornography and power.

Silverio was objective and told her that he was not only looking for eleven minutes of pleasure, he was looking for the pleasure he will have with the process. He always looked for a woman with whom he was a good partner who would help him in everything and with whom he will be completely raptured throughout his life.

Julia contested it, saying that she was already happy in those eleven minutes of satisfaction. Because what she was looking for had a lot to do with being happy in those eleven minutes. And she told him that she was connected to him because their desires were the same.

She tried to prove by A + B that love and pleasure were connected by a fine line that would last for eleven minutes. As much as they concentrated, they could only concentrate on love for eleven minutes.

Silverio was skeptical of the theory that Julia tried to show him. He contested vehemently, saying that the act of copulation with her was greater than eleven minutes. But she had a more technical argument, showing that the spark that ignited in her heart lasted up to a maximum of eleven minutes.

She could be funny, romantic and dramatic, but she wasn't one to miss a heated discussion on that topic. And they ended up getting carried away by the emotion, with her saying that he was sexually satisfied before completing the eleven minutes.

Julia showed that the main task of a woman, when getting involved with a man, is to win his heart, even if she has to go through many obstacles in her path, but she will not stop ... And she will never stop if he needs her help or he needs your support, because the woman is a predestined and brave being.

She stopped talking and looked at him and said: Do you want to touch my tanned body? And she confessed, saying:

- Since the first time I saw you at that couple party, a little spark lit in my heart. And every day that seed of love grew and grew brighter. I saw that my sympathy for you was turning into something else. And look at what happened, she said.

Julia showed Silverio that the great goal of every human being was to fulfill himself in love. That was why her goal was to understand what was the love shared with her. It was because of those happy eleven minutes that people suffer for having given their heart and the person did not know how to make good use of the eleven minutes of love.

Julia clearly saw that her husband was making an effort to touch her soul, but even so, he was unable to light his flesh to the full. And even though he touched her flesh, he felt powerless to understand her soul. It wasn't that there was anything wrong with her or him. Perhaps, she just wasn't his soul mate, yet, she hoped he would become the soul who would share with her soul the best moments of pleasure and end up spending a lot of time together.

She was aware that nobody owns anyone, everything in the world is ghostly and unstable - this applies to both feelings and spiritual values. A person in love when he loses his loved one, he will survive and that person will be forgotten, because everyone knows that nobody is nobody, and in life everything passes. As much as she wanted Silverio forever, he would belong to her only as long as the love lasted. And she was going to have to accept from life the fact that love will be eternal only as long as sex is pleasurable.

The best thing she did was to live intensely the eleven minutes of sex with her husband as if today was the first and last sexual act with him within those eleven minutes ... She should focus all her attention on him and take advantage of that connectivity and better take advantage of what she could get the best that he had to give him pleasure and joy.

Julia was willing to try and forget everything and just live today with him. They lost nothing in being whole when having sex, because the more they loved, kissed, hugged and touched each other, and the more they would enjoy those eleven minutes.

That love was not going to be in vain. They didn't meet and got married by chance. There were still many topics that they could discuss for hours on end and become truly loved ones. She was ready to carry on that love drenched in sex and many fantasies he enjoyed - spanking her ass, biting the big lips of her vagina, having her hands tied to the bed for her to hand over control of the relationship to him.

Among her husband's fantasies, the one she felt an intense pleasure that brought her to orgasm in less than 3 minutes was when they had sex in a public place, at the risk of being caught and arrested for indecent exposure.

From that day on, they had sex in an elevator several

times; at other times they had sex in the shopping mall parking lot, with people less than ten meters away; they once had sex inside the "Cascata do Chuveiro" well; and another time they had sex at the Primate's waterfall, inside the Horto Florestal.

What she disliked was about her husband's desire for them to have an open relationship, for him to watch a man fucking her while he screwed his wife, as a memorable sexual experience. At other times, he insisted that she have sex with another woman in front of him.

The voracity of sexual desire that Silverio had for sex was what enchanted Julia. It made her feel potentially orgasmic. And she started to want new possibilities of pleasure with her husband. If he wanted, she would not deny her husband's taste, as long as she felt pleasure and came, as a way to empower her body through sexual pleasure with her husband's participation.

So much for Silverio to say that he wanted to see her having sex with another woman, that she started fantasizing about sex with another woman. And what was not lacking was a woman who worked with her, wanting to eat her. She was not against new experiments, as long as she was attracted to the same sex person. But she restrained herself and avoided any approach to women with a tendency to homosexuality. She was afraid to like it and not want to stop feeling the female body rubbing against hers.

Over time Silverio stopped with those crazy fantasies that left her hair standing on end. When he traveled, she intensified the practice of sports to keep her figure very athletic. It was that athletic figure of hers that drove her husband crazy. For him, love was the reflection of sex. The opposite of her who saw love as sex with care and respect. She didn't want to be just a sexy body, but also a great soul.

His talk of wanting 200 years to make love to her was just lip service. She was realizing that he just wanted a naughty woman to fuck him. She started to get tired of those weird fantasies of his, and started to criticize him, including doubting his masculinity. And to see how far he was going to resist, every now and then she suggested that he accept to be screwed by another man in front of her. Instead of him being angry with her, he said he was going to think about her suggestion. And he confessed that he had already thought about having a relationship with another man.

From that day on, Julia became sure that Silverio was a depraved man, who liked both sides of the coin. For love, she had descended to her lowest level, having sex with him in public and sex with pain. She couldn't continue with that man who wanted her just for her sexual fantasies, he wasn't a man who wanted to build his own family.

As a test of her interest in building her own family, she asked a colleague of hers to give her a certificate that she was pregnant. That was proof of the nine if he wanted to have a future with her, now that she was pregnant. Instead of him being happy, he withered right away. And he said he was not yet in his plans to be a father. And he argued that he understood that a marriage with a child was all good and healthier, not for him.

He ended up denying that she was pregnant, for fear of losing him. She wasn't afraid of the way he fucked her in the present. Her fear was how he would want to fuck her in the future.

She didn't want to live on the edge anymore, she wanted to have a healthy life with her husband. Especially that they were in full quarantine, which requires avoiding contact with people and public places.

Since she started refusing to experiment with a third person in bed with them, Silverio started to make more trips and stay away from her for a week and come home only on Sunday - he stayed with her for a week and another week out Rio de Janeiro, as he works as CEO at the Rio headquarters and the São Paulo branch.

Since then, she has missed Silverio's warmth and affection.

It was as if he didn't want a woman who was always by her side, sharing all the joys and worries with him, he was only interested in having her in bed in different positions for him to stick his dick in all her holes. She was already feeling the black hole itself, so much so that it tore her hole from the back entrance. She was beginning to miss the warmth and warmth of a man who treated her like a woman who has feelings.

The beautiful and magical weather happens every day for those who love and feel loved. The time for fairy tales and wish fulfillment is when love happens between a man and a woman. Together they will be the protagonists of love, and they will fulfill their wishes and make themselves happy forever.

Julia had fallen in love with Silverio, like, "love at first sight". But that manhood he showed was driving Julia away.

As much as her body was always hot for him, and she always accepted his insane desire and that insatiable way he had to fuck her made her afraid that he just wanted to satisfy his macho ego, and he wasn't even there for her wishes - it was what she realized when she had sex with him.

What she liked most about him was that he never wanted to control her movements, at no time did he show that he wanted to control or prevent her from going anywhere. He expected her to come. Then he turned her on his side for that practice of anal sex, which she hated. She had anal sex with him just so as not to upset him.

He was not the type of man who liked to dominate women. Thankfully, that kind of attitude was done only in bed with her. Because out of bed, he was a kind and gentle man.

She believed he had sex like that with her to punish her, and her revenge was to have wild sex on her. As much as she felt like a predator who anticipates what she wants from him in bed, it was making her husband disgusted. Even so, to make him happy, she pressed her large hips to him, causing him to speed up the heartbeat that I could hear the rhythm of his breathing.

Julia recognized that he was a master of the art of sex. They hugged and kissed like the first time. The touch of his hot kissed lips and the touch of his gentle hands ignited her body. She even thought she was going to burn and explode with passion. And he took her fire and they both burned with desire. It was as if he wanted to show her what her real pleasure was.

He revealed his desires and what he wanted to do with her. And she allowed everything, nothing was forbidden, everything was allowed in sex with her. He was in love the way she liked it. He just put his feet inside the house and she ran into his embrace, wanting him to touch her and he slowly slid his hand down her body, and made her tremble with desire for sex. And she kissed his neck with a passion to leave marks. And she covered his body with kisses, sinking deeper and deeper, without stopping him. And the two continued with that crazy night. She was like a sweet fruit that he liked to taste.

She knew that men seek first of all to explore a woman's beauty, instead of sticking to something deep and opening her soul and her heart. For the man the most important thing was not the soul, but the physical beauty of the woman for him to be sexually satisfied. But she made the most of his desire, because, she knew it wasn't going to last long in a long relationship. She was going to need to add wood to that fire to build a future with him.

It was undeniable that mutual sympathy was shown on both sides. Her moral qualities satisfied her. He was in love, making her feel that warm warmth in his chest because he wanted what he wanted. And they both had fun. He prepared dinner as an experienced cook. And he looked at her with an insatiable desire and caused fearless fantasies and entrusted her with his secrets and fantasies, dreams and ideas without fear of scaring her. And they enjoyed that love together without reservation. He guessed what she wanted and felt her thoughts and desires. And she let him penetrate the depths of his passion. He was not afraid to express his feelings or to show his emotions;

and he gives you a male affection.

He used every minute he could to dedicate his love to her. He looked at her with eyes full of love and desire. It was exactly what she had needed in her life. What more could be more precious than seeing the happy eyes of a man in front of her, almost crawling at her feet, begging for her love. He looked like the happiness she had been looking for all her life. He looked like her dream.

Julia took the choice she had made seriously. Although the main thing for her was not appearance and money, but the human soul, with him she could have both: money, passion, sex, fun and soul mate. He was charismatic, decisive, intelligent, self-confident and modest in wanting a serious relationship, instead of continuing to change women. He was really interested in her.

Whoever said that after the couple gets married, she doesn't date is because she doesn't know what it's like to be married to a man who endorses her. She might not have been the first in his life, but she was going to strive to be the last. She was sure she was the best he had in the male life he had before her. It might seem stupid and ridiculous to think that she was the right woman for him, she was in the real world of feelings and pleasures. And she was happy with him.

She was in love. Now she felt that life was complete. And since the best way to be loved is to love, she left her heart free to love with all her strength that he would be able to love that handsome and charming man. Whether it was true love, she didn't know, but she knew that she was hopeful that the relationship would last for many years.

She couldn't have a better person to live with and share the joy of living Silverio together. He was a handsome man externally, but without inner beauty. Perhaps, because I have to make decisions without taking into account people's insides, but real life. But when he set foot in the house, he was another man and made her feel at peace of mind. Perhaps, it was so with all men who were at the top of professional success. How was she going to know, if he had been the first man, she shared the same bed with?

She avoided thinking about complex issues, such as her husband's exterior. She had more to do than worry about the other side of the medal. The best thing she did was to see him only from the outside and not worry about whether or not he was handsome internally. She provided him with comfort, warmth and reliability and sex the way she liked it.

He was always looking for mutual understanding and partnership with her, without trying to establish who is certified and who is wrong. He was a prince on a white horse, and he thought he was right. So, she wasn't the one who was going to want to get him off the prince's pedestal. As long as she gave her sex and pleasure, love and desire, she was going to do everything for that relationship to last the time allowed by the lust for that love to be eternal.

She continued to do the same things in her professional life. He never interfered with his shifts and his crazy doctor life. The only thing that has changed is that loneliness had been destroyed. That alone was worth having married Silverio. He was what he was, he was never going to change to show her inner side. He already gave her what she needed: the joy of living with him with a sense of happy family. When she wanted to be alone, she would get in her new car and drive around town. Otherwise, she would go to her husband's farm and ride for hours on end.

Every Friday, Silverio took his "Chef" side of the kitchen, and prepared the most delicious dishes for both of them to dine under the candlelight of a beautiful Italian chandelier that he had brought from Italy, on one of his trips to that country.

Julia was a woman with her head on her shoulders and did not like makeup or shop windows. And if he wanted feminine attention, she would give it to him. If he wanted sex, she gave his sexuality and lustful desires to better satisfy him.

Marriage to him could not only be about sex, but that he had hot sex that took her to heaven, this he knew how to do. She could even come and leave him, but she was going to do anything to become his lover for the sex he had with her.

Who could say what the perfect match in a relationship is? Perfect man and perfect woman? For her, Silverio was an ideal man - he was charismatic, a little tough, brave, making her feel protected. And if that weren't enough, he was successful in his professional life. He was sociable and adapted quickly anywhere. He knew how to find a common language with anyone. Most importantly, he was able to understand her as a woman.

He might not be romantic, but he knew how to understand that every woman loves to receive flowers, he always took flowers for her without having to be a special day for her. And he was always surprising her with things she will never forget. Best of all, he was a real lover. When he kissed her, her head spun, her breath stopped and she melted in his embrace.

Julia had found a man who lit her fire in her heart. It was as if he owned the keys to all the doors to enter her world of love. She was no longer such a young woman, but she was at the right age to make a man moan without feeling pain.

What she liked most about Silverio was that he was confident and knew how to listen. It made her happy beside him. He was an adult man and was not afraid to give himself over to her, who was an orgasmic woman. She wanted that marital relationship to last for the rest of their lives. They were married, so they could enjoy life with each other. She was loving having that man dedicated to her.

He put her at ease. He was not a man who wanted to make their lives so formal. He was the same with her friends, he was helpful with each of her friends. He was a man who knew how to be popular. He never refused to take long walks with her or stay with her on the apartment's balcony in the comfort of a cup of hot chocolate with marshmallows (which she liked so much).

He matched her kiss offerings. She was a good companion, did not deny fire and provided a high level of service, including affection, lots of kisses and pleasant oral sex at any time of the day or night.

How to deny fire to a man like Silverio, if she really wanted to enjoy every moment of life with him. He was always ready to walk the paths with her. The dirtier and kinder she was, the more he liked it. He was not afraid to burn himself in her fire.

She was always disarming him with her beauty and fascination. He was not afraid of a determined woman nor was he ashamed of her desires. He allowed her to talk about everything, nothing was forbidden for him. It gave her freedom to build a true sexual relationship, friendship and passion.

In that relationship, they were free and there was no place to be afraid to show their desires and fantasies, let alone show their emotions. He was always ready to open up to her and truly love, and enjoy every moment of that relationship. He was a master at giving her compliments, making her feel high. She could tell that he was the last romantic man in Rio de Janeiro. He was the type of man who was able to understand the desire of all women. Perhaps, for this reason, she would have agreed to do with him and prove all of his experiments. He had a secret way of making an unforgettable night for her. So how could she not give in to his wishes and fantasies?

She always wanted a determined man who would sometimes teach her something new, as well as help with advice. If she wanted a man with a big heart and warm hands, she did now. If she needed a warm hug and a romantic relationship, he would give her. So how could she deny it when he wanted to have anal sex with her, even though she didn't like it. He was a man of real relationship.

As strange as she thought he was, she gave in to his fantasies just because she returned the love, he gave her twice. He might have strange desires that left her hair standing on end, but he made her believe that they were building a strong and trusting relationship for both of them. His intention to build a world with her for life was clear. She felt obliged to love him, since he dedicated the greatest love to her in the world, in a perfect demonstration of friendship, partnership, teacher and administrator of that love and passion. So, how not to be crazy about him, if he proved to be crazy about her.

As if it weren't enough for him to be kind and loving, he was sexy and handsome, and there was a way about that manly man who needed a woman who was ready to share with him all the sexual fantasies in the world. He was of the following theory, that within four walls every form of love was valid. He demonstrated that he knew it was good to see a woman and touch her tenderly, hold her hand, be ready for the chemistry between them and make their hearts explode with passion. It made her deify him as a man and as her angel. He might have those freaks and fads that made her angry at him, but the next minute, she was worshiping him inside out.

CHAPTER 10 - The mystery
of the husband's absence

That Saturday, they woke up early and went for a walk on the Copacabana Boardwalk.

- I like your way, so I like you very much, she said. - It is my desire to make you the happiest man in this world. And to be able to improve your mood every day, pleasing you in bed and out of it. I want to see you always well, happy, like this. - Said Julia, certain she already knew his wishes.

- You are a wonderful woman. Not to mention the beauty of your extremities. I've never been so happy with a woman as I am with you.

- From the moment I laid eyes on you, I said to myself: It is with this cat that I want to wrap myself in his body and give my whole body to him to do what he wants with me, she said, with that look of hers of sensuality that drove him crazy.

"I needed a hot woman like you to warm me up every night and feel her purring in my ear the way you do when we make love," he said.

- Wow! It was overwhelming the lust I felt for you that night at our couple's party. I said to myself: "a beautiful man here, I liked him. I hope he chooses me".

- I didn't want to wait for you to choose me, I tried to paste it on you, before an adventurer could use you. And I didn't let go, I didn't want any of those women to come near you, she said.

Silverio just looked at her, satisfied with what he heard.

- When I saw so many beautiful women and younger than me, I felt like a rubber cat. Still, I believed I could compete with them. Then I thought to myself: real men like aged wine. I will be the wine of that beautiful 55-year-old boy. - Said Julia, she said. - I was the perfect woman for you, because I was ready to let you into my life.

- When I saw you, my eyes didn't want to leave you. I'm sure other men wanted to be with you. But I was quicker to launch the boat at you, he said.

- I noticed your look. As it was the woman who took the first step to take the man out to dance, I went ahead and went to sit beside him. I might not know you, but my intuition knew what you could give me. I almost told her I didn't suffer from a headache and cooked perfectly well, she said playfully.

The two laughed as they walked hand in hand.

- I'm glad you liked me, because I was ready to get drunk on you that night. I was open to a serious relationship and was only going to serve you, she said.

- I was the one who got drunk on you, so much that I looked at you. I looked as if I was mesmerized by looking at you so much, he said, not afraid to confess his love for her.

- When I took you to meet my parents, my mother told me to grab you and not let you out of my life, said Julia, revealing her impressions she had of him.

- I said to myself at that time that Mariem introduced us, I said to myself: I want to improve the mood of this woman in this sad and boring quarantine. I only thought of pleasing her as much as possible, he said.

- What would you like to have done with me that night, besides pleasing me, she asked.

- I didn't think of anything, I just wanted to please you, he said.

- Every woman knows that a man loves with his eyes. That's why I will always try to keep my body in good shape. I will always want to be beautiful and seductive for my man. That's why I signed up for a stretching class and pumped my legs, remaining feminine, she said.

- I like you like that, pumped, muscular body. You are a hit woman. I don't know how those doctors who work with you don't go crazy. They must be sorry to let you get away from them, he said.

- Do you know what happened to me the other day, when I entered a store in the Rio Sul mall and tried on dresses and skirts? I put on a short skirt, put on high-heeled boots and stood in front of the mirror, feeling beautiful, admiring me, smiling and I thought: Silverio will surely fall in love with me in this short skirt and long boots, when he sees me dressed like this. - She said. - Then the salesman came and said that skirt was inappropriate for my age and offered me a long dress. That was like a bucket of cold water, it saddened me. I left the store and didn't buy any dresses.

- Swear? What a rude person the salesman was. I want to go there with you so you can try on the same dresses and skirts, I want to see what this bastard will say to you, said Silverio.

- Nonsense, my love. It's gone, my anger at him is gone. Suddenly, he just wanted to please me with his suggestions, she said. - Even because his opinion will not change my self-esteem.

- You're right. There is no point in wanting to educate those who are already rude like this salesman, he said.

- Love, a friend gave me a certificate in a tattoo parlor and advised me many interesting ideas and very interesting places on my body to tattoo. I told her I was going to consult with you, where a tattoo would look better on me. Time passed and I ended up forgetting to get my advice from you, she said.

- I think it will be the worst thing you will do on your body.

Anyone with a beautiful body like yours should never get a tattoo, he said.

- Okay, so I won't do it. I just want to be attractive to you pretty, she said.

- Speaking of body, you know that in our body there are 10 secret points, affecting which obtains a wave of energy, strength and relaxation. Do you know what is most important in the massage of these points? She asked maliciously. - The important thing is to know some secrets. If you're interested, I'll tell you these little secrets today, when we get home.

- I will love to be your masseuse. I will strive to be the best masseuse; and not just a massage therapist. I will want to do more than just massage, he said.

- Glad you want to learn more about my body. Whenever you want to learn about any erogenous points on my body, I'll be happy to tell you what erogenous points for you to explore, she said - My flower needs your hose to water a lot. Only when my flower is very wet will you remove everything from it. Your pleasure depends directly on you.

- I'm ready with the hose in excellent condition, he said.

- What are you willing to do to have the best pleasure of your life? My body is thirsty for kisses and mine longs for you and your penetration, she said. - All of this is just for you, today I am very needy and I want you. What will you think for our enjoyment? Or do you want to rest today?

- I am ready for many things with you, he said.

"Then come quickly and take off my clothes, which I already own, and I will be yours forever," she said. - Let's make this night better. Come and at the entrance, you take off my clothes and I will be all yours.

- This is good. There are some details, however small, that the man needs to know about the woman's body. It will certainly help a lot in the relationship. Details that I may know about your body will bring us closer together and give us joy, pleasure, comfort, fun, love and a great feeling for both of us when making love, he said.

- I am a romantic and sensitive woman with a big warm heart, a sharp intellect, I am strong and passionate at the same time. I know how to love and I will always look for a better position to give myself to you. - She said. Always try to appreciate my inner world and feed my heart and soul with your love. Always make me laugh, never want to be angry with you.

- I will always want to be the perfect man for you, he said, shaking her hand, making her see the sparkle in his eyes full of passion and desire for her.

- I want you to always hold my hand when we leave. I want you to hold me tight and kiss me passionately and never let me out of your life. I chose you to be my husband forever. I have a special feeling for you. I will always strive to be happy together, she said, with that loving way of her.

Silverio confessed to Julia that some of the most difficult things in this world is wanting someone. He was very categorical in saying that all you can do is wait for cupid to give us a person to make up a couple. Waiting for the person to form a couple is the most difficult torture. And not everyone is ready for that. Waiting causes doubt, risk and difficult times. But anyone who really wants to be happy in love, to love and be loved, should never be afraid of the unknown. No matter how many months pass, an hour the right person will show up wherever we are. The universe conspires so that everything is done to find the person who will pair with us. Desire to love works wonders. We must be ready to overcome obstacles by a single hope of loving and feeling what happiness is in love.

When he finished that confession, he asked if she confirmed what she had said at the altar the day they were married. If she kept that same feeling when they said yes to her priest, witnesses and her parents.

With a suspended breath, she said yes, embracing him warmly and kissed in the middle of the Copacabana Boardwalk, while people passed by and applauded that loving attitude.

After they broke away from that cinema kiss, they continued on their way. It was as if this morning was meant for both of them. They came to love that morning that seemed to smell amazing.

- Do you know anything better than a love morning like today? It seems like there is a breath of pure air blown just for the two of us, carrying our energies for our love to become stronger, she said.

"The magic of love is second to none," he said.

- I think there is something that will make us much better, do you know what it is? Going to our house to make love and then making our delicious lunch, what do you think? She asked.

"I will be very grateful for that," he said.

Julia loved romance. She thought that having that romance with her husband was the most wonderful feeling between them. It is at that time that time stops and only two people remain together. At that time when the eyes look at each other, everything is clear without having to speak a word.

At that time, between four walls, it is time to kiss and touch with great expectations. Man and woman touch each other and each other's lips meet and everything stops. Perhaps, that is why they say that souls are on the lips of lovers. Anyone loves these moments of love.

Julia and Silverio didn't get tired of experiencing it all between them. That was a feeling that they liked to experience those feelings inside their room. It was what brought them closer to each other.

They made a perfect match. They were open, loving, romantic and considerate of each other. With that, they were more positive, they smiled more and showed how much they loved each other. He was her man; and she was his wife. He was her best friend with whom she could share every moment of her life ... with whom she could share all of her love and pleasure, joy and happiness.

Silverio shared with her his passion and the fire of his soul. When the night came and made everything dark, she was not afraid because she can protect herself in the embraces of her husband who gave her love. Her heart was always full of tenderness and love for her. They helped each other find happiness and enjoy time together under the blanket, making that night cozier.

Without prefaces, the two recreated that love relationship daily, learning from each other how to make themselves happy. It was as if every day they admitted in their lives that each was ideal for the other. She was capable of infuriating the ocean of passion just to feel the love he felt for her. He was capable of spontaneous actions to take you to the roof of a skyscraper to make love. She was ready for that.

She had never found the word "love" as beautiful as she did now. If before she thought the phrase "I love you" was just a phrase to decorate the relationship because nobody proved what people said, she now believed in love. She felt true love in her relationship with her husband.

Not that she saw love as beautiful as in books, but a love between people who live reality. She had a man beside her, without fantasizing that love is forever, as in books. She was going to love her husband until he cheated, because he was going to cheat on her, no matter how long it took, one day her body would not attract him as she does today. But she wasn't going to suffer in advance. May that love be eternal while the lust and desire for sex lasted. If he betrayed her, she would not be the only woman to be abandoned by her husband. So, she lived today beside him, without jealousy and without fear that he would one day betray her.

Julia was terrified of a jealous man. Jealousy haunts people. Jealousy is harmful to relationships, which, in his opinion, jealousy destroys love. She saw no reason for anyone to be jealous of a loved one, because how could anyone be jealous of the person she trusts with my heart. Jealousy for her was an indicator of a lack of confidence in the sincerity of the feelings of a loved one. For her, jealousy cannot bring anything good to a relationship with strong feelings, other than anger and resentment. Because jealousy affects relationships negatively.

Everyone says that women should always be affectionate. She disagreed that the less a man loves a woman, the more she likes him. That hypothesis was not true. She wanted her husband to love her so that she could feel the affection and the caresses that he made her every day. The more he loved her, the more she would give him more love. This is because, the woman is the reflection of the love that the man gives her. If he gives you little love, she'll start killing him in your heart. One day she decides to leave him and go to live with another man who gives him more love, more affection, more caresses and oral sex.

Love is the greatest currency that governs the world, because nobody can buy it or steal it, it can only conquer it. When a couple loves each other, no flaws in their loved one will be noticed. So, if her husband, like her, continues to believe in love, they will never be separated.

Julia was a practical woman, while still being romantic. She always needed a real touch, lots of sweet kisses and warm hugs from a man. So, when Silverio proposed marriage, she didn't think twice, she accepted it right away, because he was proposing to build a relationship for the future.

Julia never had a vocation to be a lover, only to be a wife and mother.

CHAPTER 11 - The Happiness Dream

Julia was in a complete state of happiness. Silverio had stopped making those indecent proposals. And he started to make real love to her, completing her feminine side. The sex he gave her was the best sex she could have with him. She found it incredible when two lonely but kind hearts meet among thousands of people. They had been graced by the fate that brought them together and brought them together.

The way he gave himself to her in bed was real. It was as if a volcano was sparking her heart. The attraction crossed her body and he had sex with her in all positions. It was like he wanted to rip every hole in her body. What she liked most was that he always started with caresses and passed that ox tongue in her vagina up to her anus, leading to the madness of pleasure.

He looked at her like no man looked at him. It was a look of passion and confessional desire, as she had never experienced before. Everything with him was like the first time.

She had hooked him. She wanted as much as he could give her. She saw in the world of the moon, so much that she was in love with Augusto Silverio.

There was sympathy and mutual attraction between the two. They wanted to be together all the time; and even sleep together to spend more time together in love.

The hours, the days, the weeks were his allies. When they were together, they did not detach from each other. Love played in their bodies. They didn't have a single place to mate.

Julia now felt the pleasure of providing her daily experience with her husband; and he with her. She was very active and insatiable for sex with him. The more she wanted, the more he liked her with pleasurable sex.

Weekends were fun, with walks, picnics, walks on the Copacabana boardwalk, but Julia felt so exhausted after being on duty at the Lagoa hospital that she just wanted to sleep. Perhaps it was a lack of praise from her man, since her husband was traveling to São Paulo and would stay there all week.

It could only be lack of praise, since praise is like the sun for the sunflower. A praise works to elevate her sexual power, it is as if she were connected to the power outlet. Then she lit the volcano that showed that she wanted sex. The way was for her to pick up her toys and masturbate.

She was no different than other women who depend on the man's opinion of their curves and their extremities. After having loved each other, she was elated. But she still needed those compliments that men insist on saying: that she was sexy, hot and those things that every man says to enhance the woman's ego. She would be lying if she said she would rather hear that she was smart, a good wife, etc. What she wanted to hear was that her body was pure lust, that her body was beautiful, but that her body edges were a real sin of the flesh.

Maybe, that's why she thought she was a good couple with Silverio. He spared no praise for her body edges. She thought they were an incredible couple. They had enough sensuality to be attracted to each other.

When they went out and strolled in the Rio Sul mall, people would turn around to look at them. Perhaps, they thought: "oh, what a beautiful couple". The men looked up to admire her sculptural ass. She had already gotten used to those men's attitudes. Cariocas are crazy about asses. The woman may be ugly in face, but if she is beautiful in body and good on her ass, they are happy with her.

Julia remembered a phrase she had seen in a furniture

store, she didn't know where, but she didn't forget the phrase she had as a slogan on the King-Size bed: "Do not break your wife's heart, better break the bed by doing love".

It made her think of her old boyfriend, who didn't need much effort to satisfy all of her intimate needs. He used to say she was pure sin of the flesh that made her satisfied horny. It was there that she found the saying: "happy man is when he makes his wife come and be satisfied".

This time, he had outdone himself by having sex with her. He had really made love to her. Maybe because he was going to travel and would be away from her for a week. It was as if he wanted to make her understand that she wanted to spend her whole life with her. That attitude of "making love" to her before traveling was a message for her not to feel her bed empty and cold, because he was going to come back and have the best sex of her life.

So, she wouldn't ignore the destination, she would wait for him and when he returned from the trip, she would give the best sex and in the position that he wanted to penetrate her.

Julia had gone to take Silverio to Santos Dumont Airport, in downtown Rio, for him to embark for São Paulo. When she returned home, she hit a longing that she could not discern what in fact was that anguish that dominated her mind as a longing for someone.

Little by little she was taking those daydreams from her heart to pieces.

- "Today I am a kitchen slave, it is time to prepare something to eat", since I will be without my man to feed me with love and sex, she said, going to the kitchen to prepare lunch. And she took advantage of the fact that she only went to work on Monday night.

At that time her cell phone screen lit up. She looked and saw that it was Silverio. She answered, and heard his voice saying:

- Hello, my love, I've landed. Now I'm going to my apart-hotel in Mocumbi. I miss you so much. As I don't like to be alone, later I will go to the Caesar Park hotel, where we stayed there, the last time you traveled with me to São Paulo. - The meetings will be held there at the hotel. Wish me luck, I will work these days as a workhorse, he said, full of pampering with her.

Good luck my love. Take care. No looking at the butt of the Paulist's. You won't find a girl from São Paulo who has a more beautiful ass than mine. In one detail, my ass is yours that you eat whenever you want, she said to cheer him up.

He laughed on the other end of the line.

- Open the Google Maps map and there you will find a Rio de Janeiro, where there is a beautiful and hot woman who needs to be eaten by you", she said.

- I have some magic words to tell you: I love you, I'm sick of missing you, he said.

- I want you to know that I got my pussy wet just by hearing your voice. Come soon to put out the fire that radiates from my pussy and burns me all, he said

"Take a picture of her and send it to me," he said.

- Ok, I photograph now and send, she said.

Julia took a photo of her boobs, pussy and ass and sent it to her husband via WhatsApp.

Wow, you are my sex sin, he said.

Julia laughed and said:

- Good thing God didn't give me a bad romance or make me fat; he didn't let me have a bad sexual experience or join LGBT. I'm glad I missed those chances. As my mother once said to me, "you cannot lose what belongs to you or what heaven has prepared for you".

Silverio laughed, on the other end of the line.

- According to Pepeu of the "Novos Baianos", men are half female and half male. And Sigmund Freud said in his analysis of the appreciation of the two sexes, that men fall short of the male ideal, due to their bisexual constitution (male and female), being contaminated by the female due to their bisexuality. Therefore, both men and women are liable to like people of the same sex. - Said Julia.

- Don't worry, I really like a woman. I was born a man and I will die a male, fulfilling my duty as a man, he said. - Freud's theory dealt with the desire of women, not men.

- Remember that I am a fragile woman who needs you by my side. Don't delay there, come back soon, my pussy is gone and when she wants to fuck no one holds her. - She said, in a tone of voice almost begging him to come back soon.

- I'll be there on Saturday night or Sunday until noon. - He said.

- Come and I will free you from boredom and lack of sex. I will be waiting for you for new diversions, new positions and new orgasms. - She said. - No matter what I will give you, what will matter is how I will give you. Because I care how I will give you pleasure, like your wife.

- This is wonderful. It was all I needed to hear, he said.

- I need your attention and your pampering, your very hard tongue on my clitoris to prepare for penetration to drive me crazy. Don't tire your big boy with another pussy, when he gets here, he'll have a lot of work to do, she said.

- This boy will never play with another pussy, only his, as long as I live. I will be very horny for you. I want a lot of creativity to elevate our desires and aspirations, he said. - Too bad I can't feel your body and your chemistry right now, for being away from you. When I get there, I want to have oral sex on you sitting in the gynecological chair.

"I will do all your will when you get here," she said, eager to feel him inside her.

- This week we will be far from each other, but soon we will be together and we will quench our thirst for loving each other, he said. - Thank you for giving me your time to enjoy the pleasure of being one another.

- Thank you for being part of every day of my life, even when you are away from me. I'm looking forward to you coming back and covering me with kisses and your hot body, she said.

Wait just five more days. Take a beach to become the color of sin. Change the bedding and get all the perfume on, that Saturday I'll be coming back to you, he said.

- My love, I am just making a duck and pumpkin ground meat, with low fat content, you want to join me for lunch together naked. I'm already naked how do you like to see me doing our dishes? She asked.

- My love, go put on an outfit. Watch out for neighbors with binoculars, he said playfully. - Thank you, my love, I would like to be there with you for lunch together.

- I'll be waiting for you to arrive. Do you already know the time you will land at Santos Dumont Airport? I will wait for you at home, preparing our candlelight dinner. - She said. - My heart is pounding and my pussy is wet just thinking about your cock entering her.

- Keep talking, he asked.

- Can you guess where my hand is? Can you guess what my little fingers are doing? A, my love ... My little fingers are taking the turn of your dick, going in and out of my pussy. Um, it tastes good, my love. Oh, oh, how you are missing me, here, now, my love - She said, pretending a masturbation to cheer her husband up and decide to return soon.

- His words touched me tenderly and made my cock rise. This is not the case with a husband in love with his sexy, hot wife, he said.

"May it not encourage you to look for a woman to relieve yourself," she said. - You better not be away from me too long. I'm like a cat in heat. Remember that a husband should not leave his wife for more than three days without sex. The passions of love, tenderness and affection channel the libido into the main stream that flows into the pussy and there is fire uphill. Come back soon and bring your hose to put out my fire.

- No matter how tired I am, I will give you the power of passion for you. Because making love to you is one of the most important functions in this life for me. We will unite every cell in our bodies and souls for the sex we will have will be unforgettable, he said.

- My love, take care. Remember that São Paulo is at the mouth of the new coronavirus pandemic hurricane, she said.

- Yes, my love, I will be very careful, he said.

- Remember that you have a new, beautiful and hot woman. Believe me. Everything you need from a woman, you have in me, she said. - My sweet beloved husband, come back soon so that I can satisfy your male desires with my body, with my kisses, my treats, with my smile, with good conversations... You are worthy of my love. I just want you.

- Thank you, my love for sharing your inner thoughts and desires with me. I want to remain necessary for you. I'm really missing you, he said. When I get there, we will go to Arpoador beach to see the sunrise and see the sunset. There is our tiny world where our dream seems to begin, he said. - I love you so much that I even forget that I am away from you and I have to spend another five long nights sleeping alone without your hug.

- My love, I want to write with you our love story, where we can put everything we want. It will be a fairy tale that will last forever, she said. - All our dreams we will put in the book. I will tell you about myself and you will tell all your past life to this day. What do you think of the idea?

- Are you serious? My love to write stories about ourselves requires talent and an artist's soul. This is something I don't have, he said. - But I will support you. As far as I remember, I would tell you about myself and you organize the context in book form. Now I need to go. His lunch is already cold. You will have to warm up. Good afternoon my love.

- Take care. Know that I love you, my baby. - She said, saying goodbye to her husband.

Julia was thoughtful, still holding her cell phone.

"Wow! She will be married for four months to Silverio. It seems like yesterday that we met at the party of socialite Mariem Durval, the matchmaking angel. I owe this happiness to her who organized that unusual party. She is more than an angel; she is a saint. How many people has she saved from loneliness", said Julia to himself?

Julia reheated the food and had lunch. It was after two o'clock in the afternoon, when she finished lunch. She washed the dishes and made a very sweet passion fruit juice; and she drank savoring the taste of passion fruit.

That night Julia had a prophetic dream. She saw Silverio dead inside a coffin. She asked people why she had not been notified of her husband's death. People turned their backs on her, no one spoke to her. After much struggle, she woke up from that nightmare.

She switched on the lamp and sat on the bed and leaned against the padded headboard covered with blue chenille with tufted, and began to think about her dream.

"Putz, my dream seemed so real," she murmured. - Better not be trapped with dreams that seem more premonitory. I have more to do than be jealous of my husband. Jealousy only adds fuel to the fire among couples in love.

Julia called Carla Dias and said she would be alone that

night, and asked if she wanted to go with her to La Mole restaurant to eat a shrimp stroganoff at Tijuca's bar. She wanted to leave the house that night.

- I don't want to make dinner and eat alone today. He wants to see happy people, even two meters away.

- Yes, we are, friend. As I have a doctorate in cardiology, no one better than me to accompany a lonely woman. I know everything about the heart and how to treat it, said Dr. Carla Dias. - I was here sad to be alone. You still have a husband, and I haven't smelled a man in almost a year. The only thing that relieves me are my nimble little fingers that make me see the entire constellation of stars in the sky.

The two laughed yummy.

- Do you mind going in your car? I have a phobia of driving, I told Julia. - I often take an Uber to go to work, all because I can't stand the traffic in Rio de Janeiro anymore.

- I'm going to take a shower and perfume myself. When I'm ready, I'll call you to go down to La Mole. I'm already mouth-watering just thinking about eating the food they make, I told Carla.

- Okay. I already took a shower. I'm just going to put a blusher on my face and lipstick on my lips, perfume myself, put on a pair of tight white pants to awaken men's libido when they see my extremities, said Julia.

- Friend, you are cruel! Oh, how I wanted to have my ass like yours to be desired by men, just because I see that people have libidos in some part of my body, I told Carla.

- I wanted to have the beauty of your face, your green eyes and your hard breasts that look more like silicone. I only believe that they are natural because I have known you since we were students at Fundão, in medical school, said Julia.

Now, friend, and you think that men care about a woman's breasts, they really like the woman with a big butt and shaped with localized exercises like hers, said Carla.

- Friend, get ready. We talk, enjoying a delicious shrimp, she said to Julia.

- I will want a very juicy barbecue, one that makes your mouth water when it is put on the plate, said Carla. - I get ready in half an hour.

The two went to La Mole restaurant and had dinner, talked and laughed heartily. When they got back, Carla went to sleep with Julia. Even though she slept in the same bed, Julia's heart did not need high-quality treatment or love between equals for her salvation and healing. Carla would like to start the treatment and make Julia her VIP patient.

The next morning, the two went to have breakfast at Bistro do amor, by Helena, Julia's cousin. After the two left the Bistro, they went to lunch at Carla's mother's house in Petropolis. They spent the day in the pool at the grandparents' farm. She spent more time at her grandparents' house than at her apartment in Copacabana.

At the end of the day, the two returned to their homes. Carla left Julia at her apartment and she went to her penthouse apartment at R. Dias da Rocha, a few meters from the corner of Av. Nossa Senhora de Copacabana.

Carla hated living alone. Every time she came home, she was sad, because her apartment was always empty and there was no one to keep her company. She dreamed of the day to come home and her love awaited her with a very hot coffee with toast, and he whispered in her ear that he had been thinking about her all day.

She had had a relationship until recently. But she found out that he cheated on her, and left her very hurt. Her emotional state had been on the verge of suicide. But she got better and decided not to get involved with any men. She preferred to exchange caresses with another woman to forget about her ex-boyfriend. And in parallel, she was looking to find a man who truly loved her and was faithful. But for now, she didn't want anyone under her roof. She didn't want to have a man stuck to her foot, much less a woman.

She was thinking about leaving the medical career and dedicating herself only to her car showroom, selling Audi and Tesla. She had found herself in her new activity. As much as people say that women and the steering wheel don't match, she was feeling like England driver Lewis Hamilton, the world champion and record holder of F1 history victories.

Carla was not a woman to apologize or give a second chance to an ex-boyfriend who cheated on her. Unless she was very much in love, because everyone makes a mistake.

Carla was a successful woman, but in her opinion, there is no happiness without someone to love and be loved. She could even relate to a woman, but what she really liked was a man. She wanted a man to raise a beautiful family with her, who she would love and who he would love. She wanted to come home from work and find her man preparing her dinner and when she put her feet inside the house, he would bring her a hug and kiss her for a long time. She was tired of the empty house and seeing only the walls, her bed and those inanimate objects.

Carla, when leaving the shift, met Julia at the hospital. And the two left agreed to go for a walk on the Copacabana Board-walk. Then the two looked for a nice place in Ipanema to have a cold beer, and were talking. And when the sun was going down in the afternoon, they went to Arpoador beach and waited for the sun to set. There was no better place than watching the sun go down, sitting on the stones of Arpoador.

That place was really nice.

CHAPTER 12 - Woman's head

Julia loved to sit at the porch table and drink a cup of aromatic cappuccino and be alone in her thoughts. It was in those moments that her thoughts worked so fast that it was simply unreal for a man to follow her thoughts. No man will ever know what goes on in a woman's head. Perhaps, it is better for man not to know at all. Not because there is something bad in her thoughts, but because the woman's thoughts work, they go by so fast that they just seem unreal to accompany them. Thankfully, it's not the woman's thoughts that attract men. Good thing she attracts men is just what they see on the outside of the woman - the volume of the extremities.

Julia was a versatile and well-balanced woman. She was not a woman to be jealous. It wasn't jealousy that was going to make a man stay with her.

Time and waiting for no one. She wanted to be at Silverio's side, but he hadn't called her or texted WhatsApp anymore.

Julia in the morning had made three attempts to talk to her husband on her cell phone, but she was unable to reach him. She left a message on the answering machine, asking him to call her as soon as he heard her message that she was missing him a lot.

As she was on call, she slept all afternoon. He woke up just as the television soap opera started. She watched the soap opera. Almost finishing the soap opera, the phone rang and she got up and went to answer the phone in the living room, thinking it was Silverio, but it wasn't. It was her co-worker, Dr. Jaqueline Ribeiro, calling her to go to the birthday of Dr. Estela Maris's new husband, a co-worker at Hospital da Lagoa.

- Come on! I completely forgot Estela's husband's birthday. It could! Tired as I walk after shifts, I didn't even have time to think. I just wanted to sleep.

Jaqueline asked if she was excited to go with her to Estela's husband's birthday party.

- I don't feel like driving, can I ride with you? You know the day you prefer to stay home just to not drive! So I am, said Julia, trying to find an excuse not to go to that husband Estela's birthday.

- I'll spend 10:30 pm and pick you up for Hugo's birthday. Estela will be very sorry if the two of us don't go to the party that she prepared with all the refinement for her husband, said Jaqueline.

- OK, you won. I'll get ready. I'll wait for you downstairs, in front of the Porte-Cochère, I said to Julia. - I'm going to drink and eat. And those who drink do not drive. So, I'm going to ride.

- You can drink that I drive for you, said to Jaqueline.

- Silverio went to São Paulo on business, he will only return on Saturday night, said Julia. - I can't stand being at home alone anymore. It is giving me a bad deal, causing me an affective disorder that turns into a deep sadness.

- It's because you're missing sex with your husband, said Estela.

- It's more than that. It's a sense of loss for a loved one, she said to Julia.

- Credo, friend. Hit the wood three times and bless yourself, said Jaqueline. - Our parents are already of age at risk.

- It's true. And this vaccine has become a joke for the President of the Republic, who recommends chloroquine and people are taking it for fear of getting covid-19. - Said Julia. - Each people have its ruler who deserves it. Imagine! And I went back to it, believe me? I voted wrong. Every day I slap myself in the face for being such an idiot.

- It wasn't just you, friend. I also voted for him. I also had no one to vote for. He basically competed alone; he couldn't help but win. The Workers' Party was discredited by the findings of the Federal Police and its "Lava Jato", which put Lula out of action. - Said Estela.

- Friend, let's change the subject. We're running late. Estela's food and drink party are waiting for us, said Julia.

- I'm ready. How soon do you get ready, she asked Jaqueline?

- I'll just put on some really tight pants to show the volume of my extremities to make men crazy wanting to eat me with eyes so horny that they will stay on my ass and on my natural breasts - here there is nothing silicone, said the Julia.

- God punishes, see! - Said Jaqueline.

Not punishment. Otherwise, He wouldn't have done me with that ass. He should have done me with Miss's face, instead of having me with that ass. It's also the only thing that makes men look at me with desire is my ass, Julia said.

Don't be cruel to yourself. In addition to the fact that God made your body envious, God molded this sculptural ass on your body. It was very deserving of him. What did you do that made God so fond of you that he made a masterpiece and put you in this world? - Said Jaqueline. - It gave you so much and made me with a flattened ass.

- On the other hand, he made his face beautiful and even put his blue eyes, big mouth with full lips. Let's change! You can't imagine how much that ass bothers you, especially when I go to sleep. I can only sleep on my side or face down, Julia said, justifying that no one is satisfied with what they have.

- I doubt that you are dissatisfied with your sculptural ass, fool me that I like it. - Said Jaqueline. - Go get ready and I'll pick you up in twenty minutes at your desk.

Julia put on white lycra pants and a crochet blouse in red, high heels in red, to be the center of attention that night. She put a little makeup on her face and put a red lipstick on her lips, matching her tanned skin, suitable to rock with her killer look.

The buzz was general when Julia entered the party room where Estela lived. The men did not disguise and looked suspiciously at Julia, causing a certain jealousy in the wives.

Teresa Cristina, got up and went to give Julia a hug. Then all the friends got together with Julia. Estela was radiant and came to greet her friend, and said:

- Friend, you rocked your look. You are really powerful. See the look of men, eating you with their eyes. Wives are squirming to keep their hands off their husbands, who have been mesmerized by their female figure. Thank you for coming to my surprise party that I made for my husband, said Estela. - Feel free. Do you want beer or champagne? There's whiskey, too. Ah, there's the caipirinha that hubby makes, a must. What do you want to take?

"Ah, so I'm going to start with the caipirinha," said Julia.

Julia had fun and danced with all the men at her friend's party. She was offered dinner and half of the men offered her marriage. Too bad she didn't need a harem; she already had a man she was happily married to.

It was 1:30 am, the manager sent the doorman to tell Estela that the tolerance of an extra hour had ended. And the party ended at the best, when everyone had got together and were in an atmosphere of friendship as rarely seen.

Julia had drunk enough to be happy. But, under the proper control of it. She and Jaqueline were the last to stop dancing.

The two left, having no contentment. It had been a while since Julia had enjoyed herself as much as she did that night on Jaqueline's husband's birthday.

- What did you think of Estela Maris' new husband? - She asked Jaqueline.

- I admired his behavior and realized how close they were to each other. It struck me as the kind of man who respects women, he said to Julia. - He's younger than her by 9 years. He's only 30 years old. And we know that she is over 39 years old.

- Love has no age, he said to Jaqueline. - Ah, but, also, Estela has a miss look and has the body to make many young girls envious … And rich, right!

Jaqueline left Julia in front of the building she lived in and went home. She had to get on the door early. It was no different with Julia, who was going to be on duty at 7:00 am. And it was after 1:00 in the morning. They would only sleep three hours that night, if they slept soon.

When Julia came into the house, she started thinking about Silverio. At first, it was simple thoughts, but then her thoughts became more heated ones. And the more she thought, the more wet her vagina was. And she decided to take a desperate step and put a porn movie to watch. Then, the way was to masturbate to be able to sleep that rest at night.

Julia liked to explore her body to discover her areas that she could get most excited about.

- "It's been a while since I became an adult, I did medicine and studied the human body, but I never stopped to examine every millimeter of my body to know what I like, what I like most, what parts of my body I feel ticklish or what makes it tick. my most brilliant orgasm. Honestly, I'm the one who needs to experience the taste of my body and the smell of my aroma. Because I need to love my body and accept myself as I am," she murmured to herself.

- "I need to stop being critical of myself and discover the erogenous zones that I still don't know. Most of the time I don't like my lush hips. And I complain about having to sleep on my side because my butt doesn't allow me to sleep lying with my breasts up. It was studying my body that I realized that I am what I am and I don't need to change anything, I just need to discover my performance better and like myself more.

- "The truth is that I love my body and accept myself as I am. I am passionate about my body because everything in me is harmonious, I can give myself completely to my beloved man and he will thank God for the day that he coveted me and I accepted him. I will try even harder for my man to know all my sexuality and the warmth of the flame of my desires that are always ready for the eruption of the volcano that is inside me", she murmured.

Julia was open to herself, to expose her nakedness without being ashamed of her man, and to do it naturally. It wasn't she who was going to change the thinking of men who get excited just by seeing pictures of a naked woman. She was like all women who fall in love not with the man's appearance, but with his intellectual abilities and life experience. She was glad to be with a man who knew how to fuck and had the strength in his penis to wait for her to come with the penetration. She assumed that she liked to learn from men, because she believed that the brain is the generator of the new masculine Julia knew that nothing that was will be the way it was love when it started with Silverio. More than she could have expected, the changes would take place in their lives. Some changes he made were going to scare her, others were going to inspire her. It was natural for changes to occur. She herself changed her behavior every day, except that she knew herself and knew how to take advantage of each phase of her mood to walk on the road of life, a quiet hour, another stressed hour, at another time being inspired to live and move on.

Julia was no different from other women her age. She was an adult, but inside her there was still a girl who dreamed of having a big teddy bear. She was no exception. Now, as an adult, in love, she wanted her husband to be her teddy bear so she could take him to bed every night and sleep with him. She pressed him against her breasts and pinned him with her legs so he was glued to her. Her weakness was to feel Silverio's care and his sweet words that made her feel like the happiest woman in the world she lived in. She loved to fall into his traps, becoming a passionate and romantic man, when in reality he only did that to fuck her the way he wanted to.

How to say that men are not smart, if they are the ones who make women feel unique, passionate and happy. She didn't care that people said she was crazy about doing everything her husband wanted to do with her in bed. Yes, she was a little crazy to continue with a man who wanted her to accept to make all the fantasies he proposed. She just hadn't agreed to include yet another woman in the relationship because she felt jealous in advance just thinking about seeing him sucking another woman's pussy. But even that, inside her, she had already accepted. It was just a matter of time to fulfill those fantasies. When he came back, she would tell him that she was ready to have sex with three men, whether she was with him and another man or she with him and another woman. She loved that depraved husband.

With him, she would do anything to please her husband. He was her angel and her demon. He had become her addiction, her drug, her vocation. When she was with him, she had no will of her own. She was at home, missing him, having to masturbate, thinking about him. He had become her love sickness. She saw no possibility of a cure. She was terrified that he would never return to her.

Julia was in need of the wild sex he was forcing her to do with him. She kept thinking about him demanding that she stay on all fours for him to penetrate her anus hard, causing her pain. The important thing for her was to share with him her love, her body, and her sexual fantasies that she was unaware of. She no longer knew that love was necessary for her, or if it was Silverio's wits.

It was those eleven minutes that made her happy. What did it matter if they were soul mates or not, or if she wasn't interested in the things her husband did to her? As much as she repudiated her husband's wishes, she tried to make the most of the pleasure of those moments no matter how much she felt pain. The dress code he wanted was to see her naked, with her intimacy exposed.

She had become a woman dependent on the sex he had with her. She would not be able to say in words what it was that they experienced, as husband and wife. It could only be the devil's plan for her to go through those trials. She had lost her inner strength, that love had turned into a mind-blowing addiction. She can't stop that demonic insanity. It was as if there was a black belt at her destination.

Julia was feeling empowered by Silverio's trip. She was being able to recycle her thoughts and desires. She was looking to energize her soul for a new dawn. The dawn she wanted to deserve. In those days she had time to think, meditate, study about love fetishes, she was trying to learn to discern right from wrong and to discipline herself. She wanted to forget everything she had done to satisfy her husband's sexual fantasies. She was able to assess that it was not good for her body or her soul. Those days away from her husband, she was able to clear her thoughts and turn that page to write her life in positive letters.

Luckily, she hadn't changed her active lifestyle and was working hard. And she started practicing sports in all her free time, taking care of her health and body, helping her to purge that addiction to wild sex with her husband. The conclusion that she had reached was to divorce Silverio, since he was going to continue with those problems and taking her to the hole.

She had grown tired of her husband who had the attitude of a frivolous man. Her dream of love was turning into a nightmare for Julia. She received no love and tenderness, because her husband was a troubled man, compulsive for sex. This was not life for her to continue living. She had a lot of love to give to a healthy man, not to a man who wanted sex by practicing domination.

She was a woman who needed to heal her soul and her wounded body by her husband's actions. She needed support to get out of that situation of living with a man compulsive for wild sex. And she had thought he was her soul mate. And she was willing to be your support, and want to exercise the position of a host woman to make you stronger, since behind every successful man there is a loving woman behind who supports him in carrying out his role in society and in life. But she was wrong. He didn't need that kind of support, he just needed sex. He was a man who didn't know what love was, he only knew what pleasurable sex was.

Julia had come to the conclusion that she didn't need Silverio, because he was not the man she had imagined. She needed a man who was a real man. She was already 34 years old. All she didn't need was Silverio. Julia recognized that everything is interchangeable, everything goes back to the beginning. Good is good, evil is bad, tenderness is good for the heart. And that people receive as much as they are willing to give. It's simple math. Whoever wants more, gives more. She wanted to receive more love, more energy and healthy sex. The conclusion she had reached is that she would never have what she wants from her husband. The solution was to divorce her husband when he returned home. She couldn't throw her future in the mud.

CHAPTER 13 - Mute Cell Phone

The next morning Julia came back to the door. As a doctor, she worked without having time to call or receive a call from her husband. One side of her asked her not to call him anymore, because if he didn't come back it would be better for her. But the other side of her said that she was not like that, that she accepted him as he was. And by showing him that she was not a woman to be treated like that. And she imposed his conditions on him so that he could stay with her.

Julia was not in the mood to think about the husband she was missing. Hospitals in Rio were in chaos, with almost all beds occupied. The number of doctors was insufficient to meet the demand, forcing her to spend a lot of time in the hospital. The lives of people with covid-19 were saved every day. Unfortunately, other lives were lost.

That morning it had been special, she was delivered early to deliver. A woman gave birth to normal birth twins. It was a long time for children to be born at term. It was a huge happiness for Julia.

Her wife and husband were so happy that he passed out from joy. This happens, not often, but he was so impressed that he lost consciousness. That was a joy for Julia, who moved her to bring that twins to light.

Everyone at the clinic was happy with the birth of the twins, who at lunchtime she called her husband to talk about his victory in having that delivery.

Julia wanted to talk to her husband to ask him if it happened to her, if he would lose consciousness, as did the husband of the woman who gave birth to twins. But the cell phone was off. She left a message for him to return his call.

As she was in a busy working circle, she forgot to call again. Only the next day did she realize that her husband had not returned his call or texted WhatsApp.

Everyone was healthy, the children and the mother were fine.

Julia went back to thinking about the couple's party hosted by socialite Mariem Durval. Thanks to the socialite, she was able to meet a man she married, otherwise she would be single and lonely by now.

The life of a doctor is very laborious. Doctors do not have time to find love in the real world due to the short time they have to go clubbing or even staying on dating sites, however much she needs human love and affection to feel loved and have a serious relationship with. a serious man.

Julia was grateful to the angel who took pity on her and indicated her name to be sent that blessed invitation to the couple's party. It was from that invitation that her luck changed. She was able to go to the party where she met the man, she married during the pandemic that kept people from hugging and kissing.

With all her heart and soul, Julia had received that man at that party and was fortunate enough to marry him. From that day on, laughter and joy flowed like a river to her. And happiness lit up your life path to real love. Her heart started to be warmed by Silverio's love. Her soul was filled with joy and in an intense joy her soul joined with Silverio's soul, and they both rejoiced and the love became greater between them. And each person's life started to be pleased with the love that both gave.

It could only have been the work of destiny that someone took her name into the hands of the socialite to be issued that blessed invitation to the couples' party. And her dream of finding the love of a real man could come true. She was now a woman married to a decent and caring man.

Julia had just turned 33 years old. The invitation from socialite Mariem Durval was her best birthday present. She would like to know who had been the angel who put her name on the list of single and successful women to participate in the socialite's couple's party. She would like to meet the person who referred her to the couple's party to personally thank her for the good she did. If it weren't for that angel who appointed her, she was still single and loveless.

Even being an excellent woman and being able to be affectionate, to have real and natural beauty on the lips, neck, eyes, butt, breasts, she would continue alone.

Julia had a natural body. She has never undergone any type of surgery, much less plastic surgery. Her sculptural butt had been shaped into a weight training and stretching gym. She was a big-hearted woman, always ready to help people. She didn't have time to go out with her friends because of her work in a big hospital and clinic. She lived until that moment without time for love.

She remembered that for a long time she had been alone without a man interested in her. She went two more years without dating. She didn't know if it was her luck not to date those types of men who just wanted a girlfriend to have sex without a commitment, because none of those men from Rio night wanted a serious commitment to a woman, but a girlfriend to be able to have sex without commitment.

Some men she had met, they had not even become familiar with her, already came with cheap lines. It seemed that a black streak had passed in her life, since only scoundrel men appeared to date her. For this reason, she wanted nothing to do with a man on any of the nights in Rio so as not to be bored. It got to the point that she didn't think she was pretty enough to get a decent man. With that, she no longer knew how to deal with his mood.

Many men who approached her thought they were the last cookie in the package. But when they opened their mouth, only nonsense came out. They behaved before her like real idiots. Worse, they had no footprints nor did they know how to dialogue with a woman like her. It could! They just wanted to explore her body and taste her honey. Many were so blatant that they said, without ceremony or respect, that they would like to kneel in front of her and spread her legs and plunge into oral sex on her.

In order not to hear those idle immoral men, she preferred to work on shifts and not have time off on weekends. Thus, it occupied the mind, while saving lives.

To be honest, she had been without a boyfriend for a long time because she was tired of the attitudes of the men of Rio nights. It seemed that those men who approached her did not understand how a beautiful woman was as intelligent as she was, to the point of being a doctor. Many did not believe it when she said she was a doctor. They were immature men, even though they were over 30 years old.

Julia was lucky to have gone to the couple's party promoted by socialite Mariem Durval and met Silverio. He was polite and ready for a serious long-term relationship. That night she started dating Silverio. And in two months, they were married during the pandemic. That had been luckier than any judgment she could have had.

Julia understood that this man was her soul mate. So much so, that at that "couples party", when she saw Silverio, she said to herself: "Please look at me and tell me that I am perfect for your desire to love". Perhaps she had said that when some heavenly angel had said "amen".

When Silverio laid eyes on her, he never took his eyes off her. And the best thing about her life happened. He came to talk to her and they sat at the table together for dinner. And he gave what he gave: they did not detach from each other. No other man had the chance to dance with her, even though some men had the audacity to go and invite her to dance, while she talked to him. And she said with all the letters: "I already found my partner, this is the gentleman", and she looked at Silverio, showing the one who came to that party.

That memory of when she met her husband made her happy. It was those memories that improved her mood. Because, personally for her, each shift was more stressful than the other.

Julia returned home, after having a tense shift, with many hospitalizations of people with COVID-19 and other people who had died.

Julia, when she got home, thought about going to the beach to get a color, but she preferred not to take any chances and give luck to the bad luck of getting COVID-19. She preferred to soak in the hot tub and then sleep. Upon entering the bathtub, the movement of the water accelerated her libido. And she started thinking about sex, the way was for her to masturbate to relieve herself. It was the only way to relax

After she finished her shower, she got up and went straight to bed. When she woke up, she would call some fast-food to get her something to eat. She was not willing to go to the kitchen that day.

As soon as she lay in bed, she slept then she didn't even see when she slept. And she soon started to dream and found herself in a tub of light translucent foam, her hair was beautifully on her shoulders, the gold chain was beautifully on her chest, her breasts looked bigger. And a man was in his underwear, and he lay with her in a loving embrace and they had sex all day. That dream lasted for more than four hours, while she was sleeping. She woke up exhausted, so much so that she was tired; but happy.

Julia got up and took a shower to remove that bump on her thighs and that preaching of sweat on her body. She went to the kitchen and drank water, as if she had come from the desert, so much was the thirst. Instead of going back to sleep, she stayed there, thinking about the dream and trying to remember the images that made that dream so real. She looked at the incoming calls to see that Silverio had called or texted WhatsApp, but neither. She called his cell phone that went out of area or turned off. And left a message for him to call her as soon as he woke up.

- "It is the sixth attempt and the cell phone only give out of area. What may have happened that Silverio, who didn't call me or answer his cell phone. Four days without calling me, it's very strange". - She said. - Ah, come back soon, Silverio. My body and my flower are in need of you. Well, he said he was going to arrive on Saturday. Now it's time to wait and stop being anxious".

Julia looked at the time on the cell phone display. It was 2:00 in the morning. She tried the call to her husband again, but signaled from outside the area. She left one more message, saying that she was very concerned about his silence. It was then that she saw that the last time he had been online was 76 hours ago.

- "It is likely that Silverio's cell phone was stolen, otherwise he would have already called me", she murmured.

- "Ah, I'll go back to bed and sleep I get more", she said, leaving her cell phone carrying on the kitchen table and went to bed and slept.

Julia worked like a workhorse, left one shift and entered another. She works fighting the virus for several hours without a break, a very difficult situation with patients who needed constant care. Every night she prayed that the vaccine against covid-19 would be put in to vaccinate the population. But the vaccine was insured, while thousands of people died in hospitals.

When she entered the hospital, she forgot about her problems and focused on patient care. There she saw real life, where people clung to a thread of hope to get out of a hospital bed alive.

That Friday, Julia had to get up at 6:00 am, she would enter the hospital in Lagoa at 7:00 am. She had no other way to communicate with her husband. The way was to wait for him to give a sign of life.

Julia went home. She was exhausted, she hadn't pinned her eyelashes all night. She was going to try to sleep all morning, since Silverio had stayed back that Saturday. She didn't want him to come and find her looking tired. Before going to sleep, she asked the maid to tidy up the house and buy flowers and plants to beautify the room.

- The party today will be good, right, Doctor! - Said to Elvira.

- Well, if a woman's sexuality grows up to 35 years old, I'm in my age in love, said Julia.

- What do you mean, Doctor? After 35 years old does the woman lose the desire for sex? - She asked Elvira.

- No. The woman after the age of 35 is still sexually active, but she has no need for sex every day, said Julia.

Doctor I'm going to be 40 years old, but at home the bed groans every day, before going to sleep and in the morning. My José is already 72 years old, but he does not deny fire in any way, he told Elvira. - If I let him, he's not just at the front door, if I let him, he wants the back door too.

- Many psychologists say that men become more in love after 50, said Julia. - The conversation is good, but I have to sleep. Otherwise, I will not be able to stand my husband who will arrive today from São Paulo.

Julia tried again to call Silverio. But his cell phone was still out of range. Still, she left a message.

- "What happened to you to leave me without news of you? You are acting like a child, with your silence. This type of game applies when the couple is a boyfriend, the man gives his girl-friend an ice to make her more attached to him. Mass, I don't need you to play professionally to win me, because I'm already yours. Enough of that game. Stop acting like a child. This is not serious".

Julia left her cell phone to charge and went to sleep. Her heart was all filled with love for Silverio. Although she was calm and balanced, she began to despair at the lack of news from her husband.

Her appearance was feminine and her guitar body made her a very sensual woman. It would be a lie if she denied that she was about to explode, so much was her concern about the lack of news from her husband.

At that time, Julia was almost asleep when she heard her cell phone ring. She waited for Elvira to answer. As the maid did not come to call her, she deduced that it must be nothing important, that she deserved to wake her up. She turned the other way and slept.

Julia had hardened and was willing to no longer accept Silverio in her life. She reviewed her concepts and came to the conclusion that happiness should not be pursued, because happiness is always within everyone. What she needed was to re-create her own happiness. It should start with itself, instead of the outside world. That was not just a moral phrase that Julia used to say to herself to balance her mood.

That afternoon, after lunch, Julia went to take a shower. She had a hairdresser for that early afternoon. She went to the living room to see if the flowers had arrived and how Elvira had distributed the flowers in the pots. After checking it out, she saw that everything was in perfect order, better than she had done it. Seeing the house organized and clean like that, she had immense pleasure.

- "I was wrong with Silverio. He didn't even open his cell! Too strange for my taste, she murmured".

Julia called the Buffet and canceled dinner that night. Then she went to the kitchen and saw that Elvira had prepared lunch for her before leaving. She warmed up her lunch and ate a little just to keep her stomach empty. She was hungry, but it was love and sex. That, yes, was unavoidable. She needed to be appreciated, kissed and hugged. The real world needs a woman to live with a man.

Julia still had two hours to go to the hairdresser. She put on shorts and a T-shirt and went for a short walk on the Copacabana boardwalk. It felt like the air was filled with love and smelled of romance. All she wanted was for the "angel" to be with her, walking hand in hand. Even away from her, she shared a part of her soul with him with her husband.

All she didn't want to hear about that day was coronavirus. She just wanted to dream about that sunny day, that blue sea and that beautiful Copacabana beach. She wanted to lie for hours on end under a towel on the sand very close to where the tide ended. It was a pity that sea bathing was forbidden to contain the advance of the covid-19 in Rio. The beauty of that beach was when it was crowded with colorful umbrellas along the entire length of Copacabana beach.

Julia walked and let her mind fly with her imagination. Although she wanted to take her husband out of her life, however, she was very concerned about Silverio's disappearance. Not having responded to his messages was too strange. It's okay that people don't like to give satisfaction to what they're doing or want to be disturbed. But he had never been so short of news when he traveled. Perhaps, she was worrying for nothing. If he promised to arrive that Saturday or Sunday, she didn't have to worry.

She walked to Post 6, and ran back. She really needed to exercise. And a run was going to de-stress him. If she said that she was not sad, she would be lying. Her desire was to sit on a beach bench and cry. She saw everything gray, just boredom, with that strange feeling that her husband was not coming that night.

Julia did not like to be sad nor did she allow herself to be depressed. But that husband's silence was taking away his peace and leaving his heart empty. It was as if a fog had transformed that strong bond that existed between them. He was able to bring her warm nights filled with tenderness and passion, moments of happiness.

- "And if he doesn't come back, how will I behave towards his parents if they ask me why I didn't tell them about their son's disappearance?" - she wondered. - Like it or not, he's still my husband. I'll have to call Silverio's parents and report his disappearance. I will wait until Sunday. Monday I will inform them about the disappearance of Silverio".

How life is full of surprises. I now know that everything that happens in life is a moment that is soon gone. Joy is a moment. Love is a moment. Sadness is a moment. Our life is full of moments. Each person has an infinite number of moments in life: moments to cry, smile, sing and love someone. Nothing lasts forever. I am anxious, about to explode and cry. - Julia said, quickening her step to chase away those strange thoughts and sensations that was starting to make her sad.

Julia was a woman with a big heart. The truth was that Silverio's disappearance had broken some links in that relationship, she didn't know if she was going to trust him anymore after that breakup, he had done to her. To have gone so long without calling her had been a huge undo. Okay, he could have stolen his cell phone, but that didn't stop him from calling from a pay phone or the hotel. He hadn't even told the hotel where he was staying, which is common for a husband to inform his wife. That meant he hadn't been honest with her.

She thought that relationship with Silverio was perfect. And now what would she do if her husband didn't come back. The lack of news from her husband was making her furious, she no longer knew if that relationship had been ideal or if it had been a farce by Silverio when he married her.

One side of her asked her to calm down and leave that anxiety for the moment of truth. Where she has two people, she has different opinions. People are always prone to finding fault with small things. Simply because people usually count as a certain thing, they cannot imagine that there could be a setback and the person could not answer the phone, could not arrive at the appointed time, could not call, missed the flight ... Maybe there were simple reasons for that or that. However, it is natural for human beings to be offended.

Julia calmed down after thinking better about the reasons why her husband hadn't called her. What if he was kidnapped?

The reason she got stressed out like that was because she saw the relationship with her husband as a marriage that could become perfect. Apart from those fantasies of Silverio that was making him indignant, both were pleasant to each other. They were attracted to each other.

The fact is, she had become addicted to him. Maybe that was it. She just couldn't imagine life without him. All because people feel they "own" the one they love. You don't even realize that there are so many problems in our adult lives. People live surrounded by problems and difficult moments, unavoidable jobs and social ties that make us let go of those we love. Anyone can freak out and hang up the phone to not answer a phone call from anyone, not even the person they love.

Each person's motives are unique and true to you. At such times, the person acts without thinking about the pain that can cause other people with his attitude. Who could have known what had given Silverio to turn off his cell phone and not say where he was staying? She could only know his reasons when he returned.

- "I will not think of the worst to not attract bad luck", she murmured, trying not to be disappointed with her marriage. - I don't want to fall for the abandoned woman's neurosis.

She walked the entire length of the Copacabana Board-walk, going to Leme and back. After the walk, she went home and took a shower. When she was ten minutes from her appoint-ment with the hairdresser, she went to the beauty salon. She underwent Peeling treatment for a deeper cleaning to leave the hair healthy; hydration of the hair to leave your hair loose, light and shiny. And make a suitable makeup for her skin.

It was after 6 pm when she left the beauty salon and went home.

- "Nothing yet about Silverio. Well, it's still within the time he said he was going to arrive," she murmured. - I won't be enjoying Silverio's absence. I'm going to call some friends to do "pizza Saturday" at home. So, I expect Silverio, having fun with my friends".

Julia had two options: stay at home and hang up the phone and cell phone, and answer no one. But if she did that, she would be bored with boredom. She was not a woman to hide inside the house, like a bear. Even because the heat that it was in Rio de Janeiro would suffocate her.

She started calling her friends to come and have a pizza at her apartment. After people confirmed that she was going to come for the pizza, she called "Zagga Pizza Bar" and ordered pizza for ten people. And each took one to two bottles of wine to the party that night.

It was a party for women only - a requirement of Julia. Only eight of the twelve women who were invited to Julia's pizza night. As she could not take her husband or boyfriend, four of the guests preferred not to go to their friend's party than to try to justify their men that they could not take them to their friend's party. Julia had been a category, that none of the friends took their husbands or boyfriends.

Julia did not want Silverio to arrive and meet men there, in her apartment. He could get it wrong, since you never know a man's reaction to meeting another man in his territory, where his female is. She knew that in a relationship with a man there are some rules that must be followed: the main one is that a married woman should not under any circumstances maintain friendship with a man.

She preferred not to risk her husband having reason to be jealous of her. She wanted to have a lasting marriage and a long, happy life with her husband. The best thing she did was not to allow her friends to bring her boyfriends or husbands. It was a night for women only.

She was an adult and lived to understand that no man allows another man to fall into his yard when his wife is alone and helpless. She knew that men do not respect a married woman even when her husband is around, she wonders if the husband is far away and the wife is light and loose. For men, no woman is exempt from a good line. Especially when the wife is fragile with her husband far away.

Julia knew that the man is an unfaithful being, they leave a beautiful, fragrant and healthy woman at home and go to the whorehouse to fuck whores. She did not doubt that Silverio had not come home to go out with a woman in São Paulo. Now, if she knew that no man is perfect, then how to demand that her man be perfect and true to her. She couldn't do anything, just expect her husband to be sincere and loyal to her. She would never know whether or not he got involved with a woman in São Paulo. He was always traveling there, and he had never bothered to take her with him. After all, what the eye does not see, the heart does not suffer.

She was a mature, open-minded and positive woman; and she was kind and considerate to be a passionate woman. Furthermore, she did not hide his sexual energy. She was climbing the walls like a gecko, so much so that she had accumulated energy.

Julia was a woman of character and full of life. She had a beautiful inner world of honesty, good manners, romance and passion. Being faithful to the man she was relating to was an obligation for her. Being faithful was a state of mind for her.

The meeting of the friends in her apartment had been very good for her, otherwise she would have been turning around in bed and would not have slept. Her friends realized the tension Julia was in, so they were all sleeping with her

Life is one, and she needed to live today. She was to leave everything in her place and go to a place where she would not be bored. But she tried to relax and not let herself be overwhelmed by the absence of her husband who had gone to São Paulo, and since Monday night his phone was out of the area.

It was Sunday, the day had just come. The sun was still rising over the horizon between that day's red streaks. Julia woke up and saw that she had three women sleeping naked in her bed. She looked at her watch and it was after 10:00. She got up and took a very hot shower. And she put on jeans and a flower print blouse and saw that in the other rooms the other friends were sleeping and snoring.

Julia and Tania went to the bakery and bought sliced bread, cheese and ham, eggs, bacon, milk and coffee powder. As it was very hot, they went to look at the beach to see if the municipal order to block the entire Copacabana shore was really being carried out. The police had blocked the access streets to Copacabana for those who were not residents or had proof that they were staying. The beach was deserted like never before. Copacabana beach was empty. It didn't even seem like it was Sunday, a very hot day in Rio de Janeiro.

- I never saw the Copacabana waterfront empty without bathers or Avenida Atlantic without the tumult of cars coming and going, said Julia.

- Me neither. Look, it's very beautiful to see the Copacabana beach shore empty like this, said Tania. - The prohibition on parking vehicles on Saturdays, Sundays and holidays has been very correct.

- Another right thing was the decision of the health surveillance to inspect the establishments in the southern areas and in other areas, compliance with hygiene and sanitary measures, with the application of fines and interdiction to kiosks and an establishment that does not have a sanitary license or lack of permit, said Julia.

- We are living in the worst pandemic that has ever been seen, and people insist on crowding. It is as if people do not believe in the risks of taking the deadly virus, said Tania.

- The police had to close the Copacabana entrances to prevent bathers from coming together on the beach, putting themselves at risk of contracting the disease and contaminating others who will have contacts in the following days, said Julia.

- It seems that young people believe that the coronavirus will never reach them, only the elderly. However, hospitals are full of young people who contracted the virus. It is as if these people think that the announcements of the number of deaths by covid-19 are fake News, lies carried by the press. - Said Julia.

- My cousin had his car towed by irregular parking by the police and taken to City Hall parking, and he had to pay towing fees among other fees that hurt his pocket, Tania said.

We have already seen Avenida Atlântica free of traffic and Copacabana beach without bathers on a full sunny Sunday, now we can go home, said Julia.

Julia and Tania returned home, taking bread and filling it with breakfast. But before they started preparing breakfast for that woman, Julia woke everyone up for breakfast. They all wanted scrambled eggs and bacon. Some went to bathe and others went to help Julia prepare breakfast.

The morning passed without anyone noticing that time passed quickly under her feet. Julia didn't even remember that her husband had been arriving that Sunday. She took the day to enjoy with her friends. She did it well, because life flies and the hands of the clock do not stop, taking the day into the night.

The night came and there was no news from Silverio. Julia had resigned herself to the lack of news from her husband. He was very big and could take care of himself. He knew where she lived. If he came back, he would find her with open arms and he would have lots of kisses. If he didn't arrive that night, the next day she would report his disappearance to the family. She had grown tired of waiting for him. And when he arrived it was good that he had a plausible explanation and that he could convince her with a version of it. She was around here with him. A comma out of place, she was going to make a war inside that house.

The brilliant, gentle and passionate brunette no longer thought about dissolving completely in her husband's arms, burying her nose in his neck and beating her in the ear that she couldn't take any more of missing him. Her anger was so great that she didn't even think about feeling Silverio's hands on his slim body or his mouth grabbing her mouth like a mouth on ice cream. He had died a little in her heart. He would have to win her back to have that complete love from before.

Julia was exactly that type of woman who, when meeting her, loves her right away. She would soon believe in chemistry and the fact that there is mutual love. Her soft face was an invitation to a small magical world and to live in it, enjoying it, wanting never to leave her embrace.

Julia was one of those women who doesn't cry for a man who leaves her. She doesn't even watch in silence someone about to jump off the Rio-Niterói Bridge. For her each one needs to be bold and fight for her own happiness. She wasn't going to wait long for Silverio to show his grace, he knew why he was with her, he must have known that there was a marriage contract that determined that the separation, for any reason, before the age of ten, it implied a very heavy fine for anyone who violated the clauses of the nuptial pact or pre-nuptial contract signed by the couple before the celebration of the marriage that governed the couple's property regime. Julia calmed down and did not dwell on the fact that Silverio had not arrived from São Paulo.

Early Monday morning, she got up early and went to work at Hospital da Lagoa. With the chaos that had been installed inside the hospital, she forgot to call Silverio's parents' house. She only came to remember at lunch. It was then that he called the mansion of Silverio's parents, and warned about the disappearance of her husband since Monday. His cell phone remained off all week.

CHAPTER 14 - Betrayal

Julia left the shift and went straight to the home of Silverio's parents. And she asked her husband's parents for help in finding him, since he had been missing since last Monday.

Silverio's parents were not concerned about his son's disappearance. They reassured Julia and promised to hire a São Paulo detective's office to find her son. He arranged with the detective to give 2 thousand reais as a reward if he found the missing son.

Silverio's father agreed with the detective that when he found his son, he would not call him, but the wife who was distressed by the disappearance of her husband. Silverio's parents sent photos and a copy of his son's identity.

With a photograph and Silverio's CPF, the detective started looking for the entrepreneur's son in car rental companies and hotels on the coast of São Paulo. The detective found out that Silverio had rented a luxury car at Localiza. As the car had a tracker installed it was possible to see the vehicle's trajectory and its exact location where the vehicle was parked.

The detective went straight to São Vicente. Once there, he went straight to the hotel indicated by the tracker where the car was parked.

The detective found the hotel where Silverio was staying with two women. After detective Luiz Ferraz confirmed Silverio's whereabouts, he called Julia, telling her where her husband was staying. And she warned him that he was not alone, but with two women in the hotel's master suite.

Julia asked the detective to look for him on the beach and photograph what he saw, especially with the two women. And she asked him to wait for him to return to the hotel and photograph him with the two women entering the hotel. She was going to rent a jet to go to São Vicente that afternoon.

Julia went to the hotel, accompanied by the detective and two police officers from the local police station, and busted her husband with the two women, proving the betrayal committed by her husband.

On that fateful Tuesday, July 28, Julia caught Silverio with two women in a hotel bed in São Vicente. There, the marriage ended.

And when she returned to Rio, she hired a lawyer to file for ordinary justice, asking for divorce and indemnity for treason, compensation for moral damages and execution of the nuptial contract that had in its clauses the stipulated value of 100 thousand reais if of the parties were unfaithful.

She didn't want to waste time on empty conversations, since the relationship had ended, and every promise of love made by Silverio had gone down the drain.

"My marriage lasted less than 4 months," she murmured, tearfully.

The lawyer filed a request for annulment of the marriage and the payment of the amount stipulated in the contract. And a month later the judge's sentence was issued.

On the day of the hearing with the judge, only Silverio's lawyer attended the hearing, justifying that his client suffered from compulsive sexual behavior disorder, making it impossible for his client to have control over his sexual impulses, which made him always want to have partners. many different.

The judge understood that infidelity, although the law of marriage was proven and hurt, however, treason did not meet the minimum requirements for the marriage to be annulled. However, the judge understood that the coexistence of the consorts has become undesirable, motivating the couple's separation.

The magistrate cited Article 1,556, of the Civil Code, that "marriage can be annulled due to defect of will, if there is one on the part of the spouses, upon consenting, an essential error as to the person of the other". The judge found that the case of treason by one of the consorts motivates the separation, not the annulment of the marriage.

The lawyers explained that regardless of whether he was a womanizing man, Silverio was a true gentleman. He acknowledged his mistake and breached the contract he had with Dr. Julia. So, he made sure to pay double what was stipulated in the contract that shielded that marriage with Julia.

And the divorce was carried out at term and in a few days, Julia took the divorce certificate.

For love, Silverio did not want to cause more trouble than he had done to Julia. The best he did was to comply with all the clauses stipulated in the contract that shielded that marriage. The betrayal cost him 200 thousand reais, in addition to the procedural costs. Silverio insisted on being registered that the apartment they lived in would be for Julia.

Silverio never went to Julia again. It was enough for him to have paid her the compensation provided for in the prenuptial contract and to have left the apartment they lived in to be passed on to Julia's name. For Silverio that love lived with her was worth any material fortune. For, during the four months he had lived with her, he had been happy with a woman for the first time in his life.

He preferred to continue with the two women who were at the center of his separation from Julia. His excessive sexual appetites continue. He had no limits to having sex with women. The important thing was to be able to have sex with women, without looking at the color of their skin, eyes ... He had already had women of many ages, harlots, maidens, needy women and addicted to sex. What he really liked were women who liked to be in pairs to play in bed with one man. Then, he was satisfied. He could go up to two weeks without sex and without that need for repetitive sex with more than one woman.

Silverio loved Julia very much. Even during the marriage with Julia, he fled to wilder sexual practices for greater satisfaction.

Silverio was addicted to sex. He needed to have more women for sex, which is why he was looking for more partners to ease his sexual appetite.

How his work made it easier for him to be absent from living with his wife. He took the opportunity to look for new sexual partners. He was addicted to sex dating apps to find new partners.

His trips to São Paulo had been the best way for him to expand his search for sex partners. Then, he lost control. And that desire for sex became compulsive, to the point that if he didn't have sex repeatedly with different women, he would get sick with nerves.

It happened when he went to São Paulo that week. He felt isolated from the world, needy, without the slightest condition to participate in the endless meetings at the São Paulo branch. On the third day, he couldn't stand it and used the dating app and found the two cousins who liked sex with three: a man with both. He went out to lunch with the two of them and threw up his professional commitments to dedicate himself to sexual practices with the two women. In order not to be harassed, he turned off his cell phone and fled the real world due to sex.

Like the two partners, he abandoned his wife and preferred to stay with those two women for as long as he wanted and the money.

Silverio found what he was looking for in those two women who also had no limits for sex. Both had the same degree of sexual compulsion. In order not to lose sight of them, he proposed to keep them financially to be fixed partners. And he moved to São Paulo, living with them in different apartments.

Several times, Silverio's parents tried to take their son for psychological treatment to cure his sexual compulsion. But he thought that the most normal thing to like sex. He started group therapy and did not continue. He saw it all as a waste of time, he didn't believe that his cure needed to be talking about his sexual needs.

Silverio had adopted the habit of using condoms, for fear of contracting sexually transmitted infections. All he would ever want was to be a father. He said that he had no vocation to be a father or raise a family. And so, he led his life, having a woman today and another woman tomorrow.

It was what made him happy.

Julia had the look of a girl in love. She liked to compare herself to a waterfall. Inside her, the passions of love, tenderness and affection seethed, which she wanted to direct to her man. For her, feelings were more important than words. He hoped that the next man to come into his life would understand feelings like that. And when they feel the spark of love and attraction for each other, she doesn't pay attention to anything else.

As a doctor, she enjoyed her job of caring for people. She was very happy when a patient was admitted to the Intensive Care Unit (ICU) and was cured and returned to the family.

It was not because her marriage to Silverio resulted in what happened, that she was going to be frustrated, thinking that he was the only man in Rio de Janeiro that made her have orgasms. She would like to find a decent new man they would be happy with together. She wanted a new man who would provide her with sympathy and mutual attraction between them. She wanted a big spark to set her body on fire. Now that she had met a man who had taught her all sexual practices, she was not going to be guarded, leaving her pussy suffering from lack of cock. She was going to give it to the man who would make her feel attractive.

She didn't play a girl who didn't know how to kiss and hug a man yet. But she wasn't going to show herself to be an experienced woman in the act of having sex. She knew that every man dreams of having an almost virgin woman who does not even know how to put his dick in his mouth, who tells him that he never had oral sex or never had anal sex.

Julia wanted a man to marry, so she wasn't going to be a teacher in the practice of having sex. She was going to show the man that she had kept herself and that her flower was for the man who would marry her. Any meeting would be highly valued to win over its constituency.

She was going to make it clear that she was ready to move in with the man she was starting a serious relationship with. She was beautiful and hot, there was no shortage of men to want to eat her. She was going to select, and she was going to be clear with him, clarifying that to fuck her he would have to marry. As a man is easy to convince when he is crazy about sex with his wife, she was going to be the right guide to get him into his heart. After all, her ex-husband had opened all her body holes and taught her to benefit from coitus in any position.

She felt prepared for a new marriage. It could! She had had a great master of sex, Silverio. He knew so much about women that she thought he was gay. But after that discovery that he suffered from compulsive sexual behavior disorder, it was that she understood the reasons why he understood so much of the woman's pleasures; and knowing so much about women. She was wrong, he was too male to take care of two women insatiable in sex, to the point of moving in with them. It was because he guaranteed himself to be a good fucker - Julia judged.

It had been two months since the divorce was over. It was

time to start walking to find her new husband - a snake that doesn't walk doesn't swallow a frog. She was going to play with all her weapons: her guitar body, and the fact that she was the most beautiful doctor at the Lagoa hospital. But she knew that her most lethal weapon was her butt, a masterpiece made by God and shaped in the gym.

To think that she had broken up with her old boyfriend because he wanted to exchange her perfumed pussy for her stinky anus. And then it was falling into the clutches of Silverio that from penetrating her through the back door so much that she ended up liking anal sex he did. That was what she could say: "it came out of the spit and fell on the embers".

Silverio had prepared her for any man who liked women. She was ready and hot. It seemed that inside her pussy there was an ant boiling, because she was always wetting her panties with such desire for sex. She was ready to move in with another Silverio from life. She was ready to move in with another man and make him happy beside her.

Julia had an urgent need to find a new man to put out that exaggerated desire that took her seriously. But she didn't just want a relationship, she wanted a serious and honest man who was ready for a change to be a woman. Preferably he was not compulsive for sex.

She wanted a man who had the smile on his face. She wanted distance from a serious man. Also, she had put an age limit on accepting another man in her life. He shouldn't be less than 50 years old. She had a lot to offer a man. But she no longer wanted a man who wanted too much sex. It was enough for Silverio to skin everything that was a hole in her body. She wanted a man who was restrained in sex and prepared for life with a single woman. She wanted a man to find a part of her in her and she to find a part of him in him. She wanted him to see the reality and the seriousness of her intentions, and to give him an opportunity to be open to each other.

She had been divorced by Silverio for two months. She had purged it from her heart. When the memories of the way he took her did not let the memories become longing for him, otherwise she would look for him to be her lover. But she wanted distance from him, because any approach to him was going to be fire. Passion has a memory; she was not going to have control and was going to kneel at his feet to have sex with her the way he knew how to do it. She knew he would touch her; it was going to be fire; she was going to forget all the anger that he had betrayed her and she would give herself over to him. The best thing she did was to stay leagues away from him, because if her eyes didn't see him, passion wouldn't get her off her pedestal.

She wanted a new man who wanted to be her husband, wanted to be the father of her future children. Every day she would take care of him, believe in him, help him in any of his endeavors, would always strive to be the best wife for him, would strengthen his faith, and would give him strength in the most desperate moments. She would know it would be worth getting involved and loving, she would make her heart belong to him alone. He was going to make him feel like the best man in his world. He was going to be her real superhero. She was going to be the fool in love with him. She would never keep an eye on his cell phone and will get all the bad thoughts out of her head.

Of course, she would want to be his center of attention. And she was going to show him all the delights of sex. She would smile at every opportunity for kisses and sex with him, and she would appreciate the humor in him. She would know when and where to be serious and when it was time to relax and come. He would just have to like a woman very energetic and happy like her.

That morning when she was on duty, she saw you talking to the nurse about a child who was admitted to the infirmary with covid-19. And then she hurriedly left and disappeared from view.

After she was on duty, she went to the nurse and asked who the doctor was who he had never seen in the hospital. And the nurse informed him that he was "Dr. Ruitz", the doctor who was considered an angel by his patients. The nurse told the whole life story of Doctor Edgar.

She also said that he had been widowed for about three years. And she said that he had been on leave for almost three years from his activities at the hospital. And he had been working in the pediatric ward for about two months. The nurse informed him that he was one of the most competent and beloved doctors in that hospital. Certainly, that nurse even informed Dr. Edgar's CPF, better known as "Dr. Ruitz" to Dr. Julia, the doctor most coveted by the men in that hospital.

Every day, Julia arrived at the hospital looking for that doctor, but he had gone for it, she never saw him in that ward again. That left Dr. Julia burning with impatience to meet the "Dr. Ruitz". She believed that he was exactly who she needed. So, she was going to do everything to make him see in her the woman he needed to continue his life.

His dog in heat that lived inside her was always barking, wanting to wag its tail for him. It seemed to her that a little euphemism should remain between her and that widowed doctor, and that something more than friendship between them should begin. She was willing to heat him with his heat and light a fire in her heart. She was left wondering if he would want to.

But she would like to see him flirting with her and sharing her love with her. She wanted fate to lend that man just a little bit so she could share her energy with him. She dreamed of seeing his hands holding his body intimately. She kept asking herself why she needed to meet this senior man so badly, if she could have a man compatible with her age.

That passion made her believe in a "soul mate". What a mystery that a woman like her, beautiful and hot, sexy, romantic and confident, have been interested in a man of old age. But with a youthful appearance and a kind manner that enchanted her, just seeing him from a distance, talking to the nursing assistant, a rare thing to see a doctor being kind to a nursing assistant. She had to hurry to meet that doctor, known as "Doctor Ruitz", the angel of the pediatric ward. He didn't have to be perfect ... he just needed to be perfect for her. It was going to be nice if he took an interest in her, and was ready to build a relationship with a lovely woman like her. He had no idea what he could offer him.

Her fear was that when he met her, he would be indifferent to her figure. But if he wanted to feel easy and free with her, then she was exactly who he would need for his life.

Julia was a lucky woman in her life, now she wanted to find luck in love with that gentleman who showed nothing of senility, but physical and emotional vigor. It was perfect for her, who was loyal and caring, energetic, sociable and more. She hoped he would see her like this when he met her.

It was a mystery that passion she felt for a man who must have been twice her age. But she saw him as her future life partner. It would be great if he liked her and wanted to get to know her more deeply. She couldn't wait to meet him.

She was a woman who had a purpose in life. And she wanted a man who was energetic, with a sense of humor and had a strong grip, and had the intelligence to dominate her and make her a fragile and dependent woman. She was the type of woman who will always follow her man, she never got sulky and always went to the end of her search. She had a strong character, making people feel confident around her. Her eyes that were green at one time, at others were honey-colored, others were black as jaboticabas. Maybe her eyes would leave the "Dr. Ruitz" crazy about her.

As much as she thought it was strange to have been interested in an old man, who looked more like her grandfather. But who will understand the reasons of the heart? As we have already said that the "heart is right that reason itself is unaware". It was what she was feeling. She was not going to hesitate to try to meet the "Doctor Ruitz". He looked so charismatic, he was handsome and experienced, as she wanted a man to become her own. She was left wondering if he wanted a beautiful and intelligent girl who was going to love him, because she was the one, he was going to need. Okay, she was a complex, young, beautiful and hot woman, who practiced sports, she knew how to cook deliciously, purposeful and hardworking, social and friendly. And her goal in her life was to find her soul mate and build a strong, big family with her.

When she met him she would want to know what kind of woman he dreamed of. Depending on what he said, she might adjust to him, because she only needed him to be her man. For some mystery, she imagined herself happily married to him.

She wanted to be the "Doctor Ruitz" dream girl. The only thing she didn't like about him was that name. She would prefer to call him "Edgar". But the name was too little, she would be happy to hear it. For a queen like her, she needed a king. She was going to do anything for him to take the opportunity to have a woman like her. She was tired of running her little world alone. She was going to ask him to help her deal with that complexity that was a woman being loose in the world.

Her soul mate should be courageous, responsible, courageous and open with her. Because she wanted true love. She hoped that "Doctor Ruitz" was ready to give her his heart. She would know how to take care; she would never let his heart fall and break.

If he were as lonely as she, surely those two lonely souls would converge and fit together like two pieces of a puzzle. Because if he wanted love, affection and romance, she would give it to him. In return, she was going to be his forever.

Since that day she saw the "Doctor Ruitz" that she did not sleep well. She would wake up in the middle of the night to find him beside her in bed. She imagined him as a great romantic lover. She wanted to wake up in his arms, imagining him to be not only her favorite person, but also a loyal friend.

She was no different from other women, she also wanted a man's understanding, reliability, respect and decency. Then, she wondered: what will I be for him, if she was a woman who would do better every day of his life to please him.

Julia was sure that the men of the 21st century have gone crazy, they just want to be satisfied with sex, but there is little for women. The men she had met only thought of them, but she didn't care what the woman felt. It is as if he does not know that the woman wants to receive attention and give attention, a fair exchange. It seemed that the new men would feel humiliated if they met the needs of the woman with whom they had relationships. Many men are so blatant that they go so far as to propose to women to have sex with three: a woman and two men or two women and a man. She wanted distance from these types of men. She was interested in Edgar, "Dr. Ruitz", because he inspired trust, honesty and respect for women.

That week she was going to find a way to find the "Doctor Ruitz". If he didn't come to the ward where she worked, she was going to visit him at the pediatric ward.

CHAPTER 16 - The Widower

Doctor Edgar, better known as "Doctor Ruitz" lived in one of the best and most luxurious neighborhoods in Rio de Janeiro. However, the house he lived in was over a hundred years old. It was his grandfather who had built that house, when he received the land from Dr. Rocca's, after having the castle of Gávea demolished, disgusted by the tragedy that happened to his daughters and his two grandchildren inside the castle.

The house should have received some repairs and replaced some broken tiles in distant times, because the house had its walls deteriorated by time. The damage caused by infiltrations affected the aesthetics of that house that was once one of the most beautiful houses of R. Arthur Araripe. Thankfully, the house was hidden by the high wall lined with hedge of here "Unha de Gato" - cat nail – or Ficus Pumila, a climbing plant that covered the stone walls. That hedge gave a certain charm.

Doctor Edgar was the one who pruned the hedge. He was hoping to build up the courage to prepare the old walls with old plaster, worn out old paint, various spots of infiltration, mold, crumbling of the internal and external walls. It was necessary to remove the old plaster from the walls and make a new plaster on the walls to finish with plaster for the walls to receive the application of coats of a suitable paint to make that old house look like a new residence.

It had been there, in that house, that he and all the brothers had been born. That house came from father to son since 1901. And since he had inherited that house, he never had a painting done in that house. After his wife died, Edgar became disgusted and let the house deteriorate further. The garden had been taken over by the bush, which had grown and taken over the area that had once been a beautiful garden.

While Doctor Edgar's wife was alive, she took care of ornamental plants and the garden. But she had passed away, the beauty of the garden dying with her and the whole area around the pool had turned into bush.

That mansion became a haven for rats. And the large swimming pool lost its beauty and became full of mud, served as the focus of the dengue mosquito. To think that that mansion was once a place of joy and Christmas parties, children's birthday parties, parties to celebrate the years of being married to Doctor Ana Tereza, wife of Doctor Edgar.

But since his wife died, Edgar has lost his reason for living.

He stopped having a taste for vanity. His beauty faded with each lonely day, living alone in that old mansion. His loneliness and his seriousness drove his children and grandchildren away from him.

The bills for water, electricity, telephone, cell phone, internet and cable TV had been placed to be paid into your checking account, even when your wife was alive. It was the account that his salary as a retired professor at the Federal University of Rio de Janeiro was deposited. That account, he hasn't moved in years. The only movement of that bank account was with those bills for electricity, water, telephone, internet, cable TV. When the cooking gas ran out, it was not changed. He would rather eat on the street than make food at home.

That was the debatable point that he needed to change. The lonely life had turned this man into a man with no reason to live. He didn't have the strength to discover the need to find a new woman. With that, he lost the ability to deal with women.

When he finished his leave, he went back to work. Then he had to change his appearance. He shaved, cut his hair, bought new clothes and new shoes. The job saved his abandonment and changed his homeless look.

After he went back to work, he recovered his lost vanity.

He started taking a shower every day, bought new perfumes and went to the barber every 15 days to get a haircut. He shaved himself every day. And he started exercising at a gym near his home. Soon he started to lose weight and regained his physical strength with weight training exercises.

In time he started to find his home ugly. That house had neither life nor warmth. It was natural that he didn't like living there. The longer he stayed inside that house the more he felt homeless. The female presence was missing in that house, making him feel like a homeless person.

He only had loneliness as a companion. The children did not visit or call him. The pool was full of mud, serving only for the breeding of dengue mosquitoes.

He realized that he urgently needed a woman. Widowhood had left him with no reason to renew himself. Those two years he had been on leave from work were loneliness and sadness.

When he finished his leave, he returned to work at the hospital in Lagoa. Although he started to take care of his physical body and appearance, he still looked like a homeless man.

Edgar had long been waiting for a date with a woman who would make him want to start all over again with a new marriage.

Renewed, Edgar started going to banks, supermarkets, shopping malls, going to restaurants, going to Maracanã when he played Fluminense, who was his team at heart. Even so, when he stayed home, he felt homeless.

Every morning before going to the hospital, he would stop by the corner cafeteria and have his breakfast. Soon he started to rise from the ashes and became another man more active, more animated and more smiling. It was as if he had discovered a nest of green birds.

Doctor Edgar went to sleep well at night. And he dreamed again. That night he dreamed that he was dating and was going to be engaged to a beautiful woman. He woke up and started to think about the dream he had just dreamed of. Then he said to himself, "Now, if dreams are prophetic, I will soon have a new woman living with me and sleeping next to me in my bed."

He spent all day thinking about the woman in his dream. And the next night he had the same dream. And he saw the same woman coming to meet him and they had coffee together. After he woke up, he even remembered the flower he had taken for her. The flower was on the table where they had breakfast.

He remembered her smile when he handed her the rose. But he couldn't remember seeing the woman's face. He remembered that he bent down and kissed her cheek gently. And she said to him, almost whispering, "I've been waiting a long time for our meeting."

After he woke up, he leaned back against the headboard with the distinct feeling of her kiss and our happiness.

"This dream is a show that I had that woman at some time in my past, but when"? This is proof that there is a universe parallel to ours. That dream was prophetic. The afterlife is showing me that that woman was my life partner in another life. It was three nights that I dreamed of the same woman. I saw it when I went to a cafe to meet her, taking another rose for her. And suddenly she comes all pink, running in the rain, all wet and disheveled and throws herself into my arms and we kiss them. And she says the same phrase to me: "I have been waiting for our meeting for a long time".

Edgar was impressed by that dream sequence for the next three nights. The next day, he looked for a spiritism house under the doctrine of Allan Kardec to consult with a medium of the house. He enjoyed the consultation so much that for a while he attended that spiritism house, receiving spiritual treatment, in addition to taking some courses, such as "soul caregivers" and mediumship. But after he finished his leave, he went back to work at the hospital. The constant shifts at the hospital caused him to withdraw from that spiritism community and did not proceed with mediumistic studies.

With the pandemic event in 2020, Edgar avoided going out and exposing himself where there was agglomeration. All he had to do was run the risk of contracting the virus at the pediatric clinic he worked at, at Hospital da Lagoa.

He could have already asked for retirement at the hospital, but work was a reason for him to leave the house. Staying in that empty house that looked like a mausoleum was going to be a great punishment for him. His fear was to die alone, while he slept.

There was a mystery that even Doctor Edgar admired: he did not age. Time passed, but he did not age. His body flesh was still firm and his features didn't have a wrinkle. He remained youthful and with the physical appearance of a 50-year-old man. He suffered no pain whatsoever. His heart was working perfectly. His body was in perfect physical balance. He just didn't know if he would still have an erection when he slept with a woman, because he had not had sex for more than five years.

Being a mentally balanced man, he recognized that to remarry he would need an erection. But that was a concern when he met a woman who interested him to the point of remarrying. All his life, he only slept with one woman, his wife. He was married to her for 30 years.

January 1, 1901, the beautiful socialite Luiza Rocca, who had been the most beautiful woman in Rio society, went crazy after she found her husband in his conjugal bed with his younger sister. She had killed the couple's sister, husband and two children. However, instead of the beautiful mad Rapunzel being arrested, she was referred for treatment of madness at Hospício Pedro II, for being the daughter of a wealthy family. Her father, Dr. Luciano Rocca, was a major coffee producer at the time.

The truth of that tragedy has been forgotten over time, because it happened 119 years ago. But from time to time someone was found who knew all that story about the "Bela Louca do Castelo da Gávea" tragedy, and told that story with rich details, resident of the Gávea castle located in the current R. Arthur Araripe.

Edgar's father said that story, eloquently narrating the whole story of that wealthy family, known for being the wealthiest residents of Gávea. They were the owners of the entire block, including the land where the house where Doctor

Edgar lived was built.

Doctor Edgar's father said that his father was an employee of Castelo da Gávea. When that tragedy happened, Doctor Luciano Rocca, owner of the castle, disgusted with the murder of his youngest daughter and two grandchildren, he had the castle knocked down and sliced the land and donated a piece of land to each employee for the castle employees. make their homes.

The grandfather of Doctor Edgar's father was one of the recipients of the donation of the land from the hands of Dr. Luciano Rocca. Some said that "Bela Louca Rapunzel da Gávea" had committed suicide, others said that she had been admitted to Hospício Pedro II so that she would not run away from one of the luxurious residences of the Roca's and wander the streets of Gávea, shaming the Rocca.

As it was a time that the insane and alienated who had possessions were treated with careful attention and care at the Hospício de Pedro II, the "Bela Louca Rapunzel da Gávea" received adequate and careful treatment. And after she recovered from the trauma and became beautiful again Rapunzel da Gávea, her father took her to Portugal, where she lived in Lisbon, loved, was loved, married and had three children. Many wizards and healers said that those children were her sister and her two children that she had murdered inside the castle of Gávea.

Many people who lived at the time of the tragedy told their children and grandchildren about the legend of "Bela Louca Rapunzel da Gávea", that on full moon nights, it was common for her to flee the rich residence and go down the street, down the street, metamorphosed by ghost, running on Runa Arthur Araripe, screaming, tearing off her beautiful long hair that went down below her hips, naked, showing off her beautiful breasts and her sculptural ass to anyone who wanted to see it.

That story was told as nightly legends of Gávea. Edgar grew up listening to the story of "Bela Louca Rapunzel da Gávea", nickname given, because she has long hair that went down to her plump thighs.

That story survived through the nineteenth century. Each person of the time talked about "Bela Louca Rapunzel da Gávea" in her own way to fascinate people hungry for stories and legends.

Legends and stories aside, the fact is that whoever is alive is deadly: Dr. Edgar Ruitz's parents, wife and eldest son died. The other two children left their father alone days after their mother died, and went to live in Chicago, taking their two grandchildren.

The children had lived in Chicago during the time their father and mother were doing doctorate and postdoctoral studies at the University of Chicago. It is notorious the hurt that Doctor Ruitz feels with the ingratitude of his children, who never gave any more news after they left.

Now Edgar was experiencing a new reason to be sad: it was time for him to retire compulsorily, since he was going to turn 70 years old. He was only two years old to work at Hospital da Lagoa. Just talking about retirement made him shiver. How he will leave that house that welcomed him 34 years ago. There is a piece of his life. He does not see himself outside the activities of pediatrics. How he will endure when he wakes up in the morning and has nowhere to go. Staying inside that house, remembering the ghosts of Arthur Araripe Street will be a punishment for the great ones.

Doctor Edgar urgently needed to meet a woman to date and get married, before he went off.

Perhaps he would survive the retired life when he had to retire. He would work for him until he was very old and would die inside the Hospital da Lagoa.

- Suffering in anticipation is stupid. I better stop thinking about my retirement compulsorily and leave to suffer when the problem happens, he told himself, and going into the bathroom to take a shower.

- "How will I get a girlfriend if I have lost my skills with women. That was a point where he had to find a solution. I don't even know how to give a woman a compliment. Although women remain a mystery to men. I don't know what else to say to a woman when I'm with her in bed," he murmured.

- "That time that I did not practice the conquest made me too primitive. I really won't know what to say to a woman when I'm attracted to her," he murmured, seriously desolate and with no option.

- "The entire Rio is in quarantine and people are going crazy, without knowing how long this quarantine will last, if the organs that have the power to buy the vaccine from the different manufacturers are making policies with the vaccination of the population, while the case number of infections increases in geometric progression", he said.

- "Television only talked about the pandemic, infections and deaths by covid-19, scaring the population more and more". The youth who are not afraid to die continue to have fun, participating in parties without masks, kissing, dancing close together, as if they were immunized against the virus. They only realized that the pandemic is a reality and that the virus does not choose a face, that infects the poor and the rich, the old and the new, when they contract the lethal virus and their lungs are compromised and thrown on the bed of a hospital. Then, he realizes that he was lucky to get the virus", he said, with great regret for the deaths from coronavirus.

Edgar had made a list of good movies to watch. After all, he was in the risk group. The best he did was stay at home, watching movies, watching football on Wednesdays on television.

He was ready to escape vanity and give himself the freedom to travel to some park and pitch his camping tent in a place where he was at least five meters away from other tents. Maybe it would be good for the first two days, then it would be no fun to be away from civilization. Even because, he would not go to a camp alone, without a partner of happy moments.

Edgar wondered where he was going to find a reliable woman, who knows what she wants and understands the man. He knew from experience that being happy is a state of mind, but that alone is almost impossible. And her age no longer helped to win over a new woman of childbearing age. It does not help to say that age and appearance are not on the same plane. They really aren't, because age weighs in the balance when looking for a woman. Especially that he dreamed of finding a woman who could give him new children.

He always liked to play sports and specially to run out-doors. He had returned to running long and short distances to acquire good resistance; and three times a week he worked out at the gym near his home.

Edgar started to observe women better. And he noted that the women in the age group he would like to meet were mostly women with silicon beauty. Times were different, women with natural beauty were few. It made him wonder "where had he been all that time that he only now noticed that change in women in the 21st century". He saw that he would have to re-learn about the new women. It was not going to be easy to deal with the new woman.

Edgar was intimidated by the new woman. The new woman kept her body strong and fit in the gyms. This made them more energetic, making him wonder how he was going to live with one of these women in everyday life and receive their feelings. It was necessary for him to recycle his ideas about women of the new generation.

He was from the time when there were no internet and people had to write letters. People had to wait weeks or even months to receive a letter. Now everything was different, lonely people had a new, more comfortable way of communicating with a universe of many women looking for men to marry on the internet. Modernity had brought practicality in a much more romantic aspect. This was wonderful. There was much more opportunity for people to reach their passions more easily than people in their time.

Edgar had posted his profile on several national and international sites. This was going to be the school he needed to learn about modern women. And that became an addiction for him. He chatted with women all over the world on the internet in real time. They were women who offered different contexts of a reality that he did not know. As he wanted to learn more about women, he would keyboard with several women from different countries. With that, he observed that women were not linear, they remained a mystery to men, a real puzzle for men. Those internet women were real-life women. It made him feel high in self-esteem, with so many women who wrote to him.

He started to have new attitudes towards women. He learned that women look for men who share their positive attitude with them. He gradually learned to understand the logic of women in relation to desires and their passion. He came to understand what relationships were based on. He learned from women on the internet that they were looking for men who would appreciate their feminine nature and allow them to share their whole life with him. For that, he should talk more about him about what he was looking for.

He could not have better teachings on women than on the dating sites he had put his profile on. That was interesting to understand about the female soul. He learned that the woman knows that her man cares about her and has time for her. He also learned that the woman likes the man to want to know all her skills. He learned that the new woman makes no secret of her body's desires; and that he likes to feel that the man feels his touch and how much his touch excites him. He learned that the woman takes the first step because she knows that a man is shy in front of a woman.

That morning, Edgar, better known as "Dr. Ruitz", after receiving the call from his colleague, doctor Carlos Travassos, he went down to see a patient in the gynecologist's ward who had been admitted that morning. After evaluating the patient, he went to the doctors' room for breakfast. When he left and went to see another patient, his eyes landed on a woman who hurried by in the corridor of the infirmary.

He remembered the dream he had about a woman who was rushing to meet him for coffee with him. He remembered that the dream woman's floor was identical to that of the doctor he had seen a few minutes ago. He had no doubt that she was the woman he had dreamed of.

He spent an hour there, talking to one patient and another, hoping that this woman would return to the infirmary. But she didn't come back. And he didn't want to find out who that woman was. And he went back to the pediatric ward, where he worked. The next day, he returned to the gynecological ward. And there she was, attending to one patient and another.

- That pediatric doctor doesn't take his eyes off you, Dr. Julia. He told the nursing assistant that he was helping Dr. Julia to dress the patient.

"I bet he's keeping an eye on my butt," she said.

"How do you know if she has her back to him," said Margarete.

"And is there something else better about women for these assholes to look at?" - She said.

Margarete was silent, paying attention to what the doctor was doing with the patient.

- Do you know him from here? - She asked Julia.

- Yes. It's "Dr. Ruitz "of pediatrics, give it to Margarete. - He was widowed almost three years ago. Then he was on leave. And I heard that he went back to work about three or four months ago.

- Is he a good person? It is not those old babysitters who give up on everything that is a woman, is it? - He asked Julia.

"I never heard of that from Doctor Ruitz," he said to Margareth, joining his thumb with his index finger. - In the pediatric ward, before he went on leave, he was considered the kindest and kindest doctor for the inpatients and with colleagues in the ward. Patients prayed to be seen by Dr. Ruitz. I never knew he was involved with anyone inside this hospital. He is a man of integrity.

- Is he gay? - He asked Julia. - Because what you are describing are gay attitudes.

- Credo, doctor, of course not. - Said Margarete, opening that smile of white teeth.

Julia said nothing more, remaining silent, waiting for Margaret to release her tongue more. But she said nothing more. When the patient's dressing was finished, Margaret excused herself and left Dr. Julia for her to talk to the patient.

When Julia finished caring for the patient, she went to see another patient who was moaning a lot. She went to the doctor, but he was already gone. He had certainly returned to the ward he worked for.

Julia was curious, wanting to meet the doctor. But he had already snuck out, as if he stole, without giving notice of his departure to the Frenchwoman.

CHAPTER 17 - Love happened
without him waiting

Doctor Edgar had been a widower for less than three years. When he saw the doctor Dr. Julia, he lacked a stiff neck because he looked at her ass so much when she passed by. He couldn't even disguise it anymore.

Julia saw the time for him to have a pipiripaque. Before he had a high-intensity malaise followed by death, she was going to ease his tension by going to him and taking the first step to help that man declare himself to her.

She realized that the age gap was very big. She had just turned 34 years old. And certainly, he was going to be 60 years old.

She had already obtained information from him. There was no doubt that he was a very experienced and kind person, a true gentleman. But before she approached him, the ward called her to see a patient who was passing by with a seizure.

When she came back from the bed that she had to see a patient, she went over to where he was seeing a patient and said to him: "I hope to come one day to call you my husband soon to warm your heart", and she didn't wait for him to say anything.

She left him with a beautiful smile on her face, while she went to see another patient who had just arrived and the nurse came to call her to do the patient's assessment with Corvid.

After she saw the patient, she came back and went to him, saying:

- My name is Julia Junqueira, divorced, a fragile, kind, very temperamental and active woman. And I'm looking forward to getting married again, she said. - You should know that marriage is the best man-made institution. Every woman should get married to know how wonderful it is. And never even think about divorce, she said, hurriedly leaving, promising to talk more before the shift ended.

Julia took advantage that Edgar was silent, and spoke?

- I am a bright and fiery girl. I warn you; you can get burned! I'm emotional, capricious! But I can love and be loved. I am ready to make a person the happiest in this world. It is always fun and joyful with me) And I am sure that with me a man will always feel satisfied and loved! But are you ready to love a woman like me? The woman who will light a fire in your soul?

Doctor Edgar introduced himself to him, saying:

- My name is Edgar Ruitz, widowed and unimpeded, ready

for a new love to get married. - He said. - I hope it's up to you. I am also against divorce. People getting married should give up vanity, pride and hurt, and never want to get divorced, he said.

- How long were you married? And how long have you been a widower? She asked.

- I have been married to the same woman for 30 years, 2 and a half years that I am a widower - he said.

- I was married about 4 months. I have been divorced for 35 days, she said.

- Why did you spend so little time married? He asked, surprised.

- My husband preferred to be with two women than to have only one woman with him. I caught him with two women, she said.

- Come on! This is what I call a greedy man, said Edgar.

- I'm not sorry anymore. I took Silverio out of my heart a long time ago, she said. - I appoint you the commander of all spaces of my heart.

From that day on, they started drinking coffee in the hospital canteen. In the middle of the conversation, she asked him an unusual question.

- Do you think I'm nice, beautiful or just hot, she asked, placing her hand on top of his.

- I cannot give you a compliment in a single predicate, because you are all wonderful. If you allow me, I would like to prepare breakfast for the two of us soon, at the opening of my renovated house - He said, with the dirtiest face.

- When you call me, I'll be ready to go. I am free and unimpeded, there is no man on my feet. And I need a boyfriend to marry, she said. - How do you spend your time in these quarantine and lockdown days and nights?

- When I'm not in the hospital, I'm confined at home to protect myself from the coronavirus. I am in the risk group, I must not expose myself to danger for free, he said.

- When you can go out to dinner, she wanted to know.

- Today is Friday. Do you think tonight will be appropriate for us to go to a good restaurant to have dinner and talk? He asked.

- It seems to me that it will be a hot night. And if we're lucky, we'll see the stars in the sky, she said. - I'm serious, Edgard. Fridays were for meetings. I will be ready at 10 pm, waiting for you, she said, and wrote her address on a prescription sheet and handed it to him and hurried off to answer the call from the infirmary.

Julia disappeared inside the hospital. Edgar kept the paper in hand, then put the prescription sheet in his wallet so he wouldn't lose it. That was Julia's address.

That morning, Julia didn't cross Edgar again. She looked for him before finishing her shift, but as he had surgery, she left. When he arrived at her residence, she showered and went to the salon to have a relaxing massage, wash and do hair, manicure and pedicure, eyebrows, makeup and hairdo. She wanted to get the hospital smell out of her hair. She spent the whole afternoon in the beauty salon to look beautiful for her charming old man and very well physically.

Edgar seems to have always lived-in formaldehyde. It didn't even look like he was going to be 70 years old. He had the appearance of 50 years old, which impressed her when she learned of his chronological age.

It was half an hour before 10 pm, when her cell phone turned on the display. She looked and saw that it was her gallant. She answered her cell phone and confirmed where she lived. And she asked him to let her know when she was coming so he could come down and wait for him at the entrance to the building she lived in.

The two went to have seafood dinner at the "Camarada

Camarão" restaurant, in Botafogo, a cozy atmosphere, I mean from a meeting of a VIP couple. The pleasant conversation continued through the night, enchanting Julia. She did not remember having a frank and friendly conversation with Dr. Edgar Ruitz. Her curriculum was enviable: clinical doctor, doctorate and postdoctoral fellow at the University of Chicago, USA. He had been Full Professor at the Federal University of Rio de Janeiro. And if that weren't enough, he played the piano with great distinction.

Julia was impressed with the resume of her would-be husband. It was really incredible. What she liked most about him was his humility and the way he treated people and patients at the hospital. Everyone liked him. Patients called him "Doctor Ruitz".

What kept Julia captivated was that she had never heard of the "Doctor Ruitz" of the pediatric unit, if she worked at Hospital da Lagoa for more than eight years, since she had graduated in medicine. It was as if fate hid it from her to present it at the right time. And this was the moment. And there are still people who don't believe in fate. The proof was there, in front of her. So, she wasn't going to be stretching that relationship for long, she was going to lead that relationship to her marriage to

"Dr. Ruitz ". He was the guy, the right man for her.

- Due to my chronological age, I am already too old for a woman like you. But physically and mentally I feel in a position to have a wife like you, he said. But I am ready to take a "no" from you. I will understand your reasons, he said, with all your politeness.

- Why would I say "no", if I practically harassed you, she said. - I am incredibly attracted to you. When I first saw it, a spark lit my heart. Each day it gets brighter. My sympathy for you turned into something else.

Edgar just listened to Julia. He was enchanted by her beauty - physical, soul and heart.

- Since that day that you came to me and greeted me, my task became to win your heart, he said.

- I think about you minute by minute. I started going to your unit more just to see you, he said.

- I promise I will never hurt you ... I will support you if you need me, said Julia.

- I know that. You inspire love and passion, sincerity and fidelity, he said.

- Often, women are associated with beauty, sophistica-tion, charm, which is a fact. But who has ever wondered what is the secret of such special female beauty? I only understood this when I was alone ... A woman's beauty is in her man's love; in relation to her, in the fear and expression of her eyes, she said.

- I agree with you. Women become the most beautiful, strong, patient, caring, especially when they feel loved and desired. No makeup and perfume can make a woman look so beautiful when she wants to have sex with her beloved man. It is a fact that a man's love makes a woman's beauty reflect, he said

- Edgar if you had a time machine, what time would you go to? For the past or the future, she asked.

- To the past to correct all my mistakes and not make them again, he said. - And you, if you had a time machine, when would you want to go?

- For the future. To see what you became after you met me, she said. - But, probably, I would stay in the present to enjoy every day by your side and make you happy with my love and my dedication.

- I always wondered if there is life after death. I studied the spiritism book of the medium Allan Kardec, and even took some mediumistic courses, but the conclusion I reached is that I have a gift for spiritism. But I was very impressed with the spiritism doctrine. And you, what do you think? Do you believe that if two loving people were happy in another life, they will come back to be together in a new incarnation - he asked?

- I am not aware of Allan Kardec's spiritism doctrine, I know what lay people say. But I believe that these people who disembark go somewhere, because the spirit never dies, it renews itself to eternal life. And one day he reincarnates and returns to earthly life to pay for what he did wrong in other lives. I do not believe that people are born unborn or die to die. Each person's life is to adjust to God's purposes. - Said Julia, jealous of her mission in this life.

Edgar looked at her, as if he wanted to discover her soul through her eyes, since her eyes are mirrors of the soul.

- What is it? Did I say any nonsense? - She wanted to know.

"No. You are a wise woman," he said. - You have a lot of luggage to share what's in your soul. I want to say that I am not here, having dinner with you, just for fleeting flirtation, but to learn about you, for being a great woman and sinking into the heart of your soul. I'm asking you for support and your love, because your light years away from me.

- Seriously! I want a man to be my partner and live with him so I can be his last wife. To travel through this world of my God, to see forests with lush green, flowers of different types and colors, to travel to know mountains and parks ... Finally, to spend winters and summers beside my man. And growing old with a person who loves me as himself, she said.

You are very beautiful. What good will you have done in another life for God to have honored you with this physical, intellectual beauty that you have today in the 21st century? - He said. - I wanted to be a diviner to guess something about your future.

- To guess about my future and we are living in the present. The future does not matter to anyone, because we will always be in the present. The future will be when I go from this to another life. I want to live today; the future belongs to God. - She said.

- I would love to travel on a direct flight to a desert island, where I will have to merge into a tribe, where I will have to live without clothes. Such a tribe I would call "gentle in love", where they teach me all their knowledge a secret technique that will give a woman a lot of happiness with just a touch of love. If you want to go with me, I will learn how to love you to make you happy forever. - He said.

- I have kept a secret from my body for a long time. But the time has come to reveal the truth. I'm not a girl anymore and

I'm not shy anymore. If you want to live with me, I will send the code for you to access my heart. Do you want? She asked. - Let me know you in depth and when you are ready and sufficiently in love with me, I will let you know all my secrets and the beauty of my body. Do you want?

- Yes, I want to know everything about you, your desires, your dreams and all your fantasies. I also want you to be my talisman, he said. Yesterday I watched a movie about Aladdin. Then I kept thinking, I would like to become a genius and do good and seductive things to win you over. Tell me what you dream about, maybe I can make your dreams come true, he said.

- Well, my height is much higher than the average height of women in Rio - 1.75 centimeters, so I was constantly provoked at school. The boys called me "giraffe girl". That kept me from wearing high heels for a long time. I cried many times for being a tall woman. People told me that I was going to have a hard time finding a husband. So, if I found the magic lamp, I would ask to be 1.70 cm tall; get married and have children, she said.

- As a genius I will see you with 1.70 centimeters; I will marry you and give you beautiful children, he said.

The two laughed and hugged, and he kissed her.

- I really don't care how tall the man is with me, but I want to know your opinion about me, she wanted to know.

- You are a beautiful woman, you are perfect from head to toe and, you have every chance of marrying me. You just have to accept my engagement request to get married in less than two months, he said.

Julia looked at him to assess his body language.

- You want to know all my skills. I am your genie inside your magic lamp, said Julia. - Make three requests to your genie.

- I want to love and make you all mine. And never ask for a divorce and be faithful for as long as our love lasts, he said.

- I'm ready to do what you want today. How much will my touch excite you? Where will you want me to touch you? Which part of my body do you want to start kissing? You have the magic lamp, just ask and the genie will answer. - Said Julia, wanting to know even what he had in mind to own her.

- I want you to start sleeping with me every night, starting today. Accept to marry me and give me beautiful healthy children, he said.

- Are these your three orders? You don't want to change orders or order order, do you? - Asked the genie.

"These are my three requests," he said.

- Edgar have you ever heard someone say: "you put the

oxen in front of the cart." - She said. - That's what you did. First you said you want to eat me. Let's take the step each time and in the right order to make our union real and legal.

- Marrying you is what I really want. - He said.

- Edgard I want you to know that I will only sleep with you after we get married. - She said. - Our common future will depend on real and responsible actions. So first we will get married to make your right to eat me any time of the day or night, in whatever position you want, she said.

- Okay, I got it right. I ask you, are you asking me to get married? she asked.

- Yes, I am. We are adults and able to assume our responsibility to the society in which we live. I want to marry you in civil and religious terms, she said. - I will love to make you feel special and warm with me. I want to be the woman of your life.

Edgar was in shock, thrilled. He never thought he would be at a loss as to what to say in front of a woman. The fact is, he was.

- Are you ready to change your life and end 2020 in the most unforgettable way, married to a woman who will be dedicated to you day and night? Just you and me. - Said Julia. - Or do you prefer that I remain your girlfriend, living in my house and you in yours, having your bed only yours?

He only listened to what Julia said, as if he were in the world of the moon, so much was his adoration for that woman.

- I see many men who live alone, without having a chance to have a dedicated and loving woman who gives him love, affection and company, for not wanting to share the roof he lives in, he said to Julia, in a soft tone.

Edgar woke up from his reverie and came to himself.

- You know I always adore you. It all happened unexpectedly. We are getting off to a great start and I would like this story to become special for both of us, he said.

- I have many dreams to fulfill. Will you help me to fulfill my love dreams? She asked. - I want your support to help me with this. What can I do for you to put me in paradise?

- We can create this paradise, especially for both of us, he said. - The ideal that we should start from today.

- I think so too, she said. - I'm dying to feel your first kiss on your bed, your first touch with your tongue on my pussy, our first night together, our first breakfast together. But that cannot happen without formalizing our union. - She said. - How soon can we get married so you have the right to do all this to me?

- Tomorrow we will go to the registry office and mark our civil and religious wedding day. In 30 to 45 days, we will be married, he said.

I am already telling you that I will not marry you under such a stable union contract. For me, such a stable union is just an arrangement for people to officiate that they are lovers, she said. - Since we are going to make our union official, it will have to be in black and white, actually marry, in civil and religious terms.

- Weren't you married to the religious? He asked.

- No. Silverio had already married in the religious and was divorced. I only have one chance to get married in the religious, marrying you with the priest saying "you can kiss the bride".

They laughed.

- Can I kiss my fiancée now? He asked.

- A little kiss. The kiss can only be given when the priest says: "you can kiss the bride", she joked.

That Monday, they went to a registry office and she took two witnesses and arranged for the civil and religious wedding. They handed over the documents and we will sign the documents to run the proclamations for them to get married in the civil and religious. When they left the registry, they went to the H. Stern store and ordered the wedding rings. And he gave Julia a yellow gold ring with diamonds. And they got engaged that night, at Masserini Osteria di Mare, on Av. Vieira Souto.

- I want to discover the taste of our love as married to you ... The love that can only be created with you and me, he said.

- I have a very sweet taste. I'm sure you'll love to taste my taste, she said, looking him in the eye, maliciously.

- I want to know your taste and find out how you will make love to me. - He said - One thing I am sure, I will never forget your first kiss when we are making love. I will never forget our first moments together as a couple, he said.

- You are very kind. I will love you forever, she said. - Life is so short and time flies so fast, when we see the time has passed. I wish we could feel loved at every moment of our lives, she said, showing how much she was interested in him.

Edgar gave Julia space to say what she had in mind.

- I know this will be possible, because I think our compatibility is very good, she said. - I want to believe that our chance has come to be each other. I would love to feel that you are in love with me, go hand in hand with you and enjoy ourselves.

- Are you really ready to have a man who is twice your age? People will blame you for being married to a man a lot older than you. They will be able to ask if I am your father, he said, in a good mood.

They laughed heartily.

"Are you going to be upset or are you going to be proud of having a woman like me by your side, killing the envy of men who see us together as your wife?" She asked.

- Honored to be your husband, he said. - And will you call when someone asks if I'm your father?

- Do you think a woman like me will be listening to what people will say about my relationship with you? I am a passionate woman and I am not afraid of my desires. Want to see? - She said, giving a kiss on his mouth, there, for everyone who was in the restaurant to see the kiss she gave him.

- I like it. I liked your soft lips so much, he said.

- Maybe you think I'm crazy ... but yes, I'm crazy about you. I'm dying for you to call me "my wife" and for me to wear a wedding ring on your finger, she said. - I can't wait for the priest to say: "you can kiss the bride".

I can no longer stand to live in that house alone. My bed is empty every night, he said. - I don't like sleeping alone. I need my second half in my bed.

Julia went to the point and said:

- Love is made for two. I cannot do this alone. So, I haven't been sleeping well. And the conclusion I came to is that I need you with me, she said.

"It seems to me that we can improve each other's sleep," he said, stroking her hair. - Are you ready to drop the vanity and give yourself freedom and serenity to become my wife and dedicate yourself only to me in love? Remember that I will grow old and leave you a widow. But when I die don't cry for me. Get married soon so as not to be called the widow of "Dr. Ruitz".

They laughed; in a joy she had never felt.

Edgar was not happy to hear that fantastic, beautiful and hot woman. He had in mind that every opportunity for love is worthwhile, just don't fear, act and love. He had in mind that people should enjoy every moment that is good for them. He was really ready to spend precious days and nights with that beautiful and sophisticated woman, and wake up every morning, feeling the fragrance of her hair, and enjoy the many other beautiful things they could do when they woke up together.

- My interest in becoming a couple in love has been great, she said.

- I would say that it is really the destiny that united us. Because the day I saw you, my whole body shook and something took over my heart. Was love. - He said.

- Me too. Every day I was waiting for you to go to the gynecology clinic to look for me just to look at me. I thought it was so romantic, she said. - Please do not let the romanticism cool down after we are married. Without romanticism, there is no marriage that lasts. A woman needs to be courted, praised, admired ... and kissed on all parts of her body.

- Many people say that life without a relationship is normal, not for me. How can it be normal, if I cannot give or receive love? Thank God I found you to build our future together, he said.

- I loved that you were not afraid of love with me, she said.

- Who said I wasn't afraid of you? I shivered when you came near me. My voice didn't come out, I crashed. He spoke.

- It didn't seem. I felt that you were very naughty. You didn't take your eyes off my ass to the point where the nursing assistant who was helping me with the patient notices and warns me, she said.

- Speaking of your butt, God was very audacious when he made you the hottest bourgeois in Copacabana, he said.

- Keep thinking I'm hot and never stop harassing me, she said.

Edgar looked at Julia, without saying a word, as if he was

hypnotized.

What's it? - She asked - Did lipstick stain my mouth?

- No. You look perfect, he said. - I'm just admiring your feminine beauty.

Before she said anything, he said:

- Julia, we can go to the registry office on Friday, instead of Monday, because on Friday I will open my house, which has been completely renovated, from plastering, changing tiles and new ceilings, new furniture, TV room. ... I want you to know that I remodeled my house to impress you.

- Seriously! Why didn't you tell me before? I would have loved to participate in your ideas. You surprised me; you see! - She said, stroking his face and looking into his eyes.

"I wanted to surprise you," he said.

Edgard's house received new paint, the walls received a new welcoming look, curtains installed from ceiling to floor, along the entire length of the wall, giving the feeling of a large window. Inside the house new wood and masonry coverings were made to give more comfort to the living environment. The pool received a new touch-up and changed the coverings, received new water and adequate treatment.

The barbecue was moved to the back of the land, away

from the pool so that women would not be bothered by the looks of men in bikini. The place occupied an area of 150 m2, with a modern structure, closing the sides with glass that protected from rain and wind; barbecue floor covered with non-slip pads that extended to the pool area. However, the pool deck was set back so whoever was on the grill didn't see who was in the pool.

The barbecue was moved to the back of the land, away from the pool so that women would not be bothered by the looks of men in bikini. The place occupied an area of 150 m2, with a modern structure, closing the sides with glass that protected from rain and wind; barbecue floor covered with non-slip pads that extended to the pool area. However, the pool deck was set back so whoever was on the grill didn't see who was in the pool.

The TV room was carefully maintained so that the flat-screen TV was not in front of the windows, preventing the brightness of the lighting from interfering with the TV environment. Another meticulous care was with the height and position of the TV in relation to the sofa.

The order was to prioritize comfort to give lightness to the TV environment with home theater, transforming the living room into a cinema room inside the house. Leather-covered armchairs replaced the existing sofa.

Architects and interior designers have transformed the faded old house into a new house full of life. After all, he was taking a new woman into that house. He had to offer her the best for her to live there. It was the least he could do to be the warmth of a new love and new dreams of a new married life.

The month of December 2020 began, on December 19, they were married in the civil and religious. The wedding was held in Doctor Edgar's new home, better known within the Lagoa hospital as "Dr. Ruitz ".

The month of December 2020 began, on December 19, they were married in the civil and religious. The wedding was held in Doctor Edgar's new home, better known within the Lagoa hospital as "Dr. Ruitz ".

The back areas of the house had been prepared for the wedding of the mansion owner. The areas that were part of the pool were covered with non-slip ceramic, where the altar was going to be set up and the chairs were placed for the guests for the wedding of the newlyweds "Doctor Ruitz & Doctoral Julia.

That Saturday, the last preparations for the wedding were made: Religious ceremony, with Father Eustáquio de Melo as celebrant. Organized the accents for the guests, taking care to take into account the number of guests. Decoration / florist at the groom's residence. Music, Photo / Filming. Beauty salon for bridesmaids separated from the bride. Preparation of the bride with the wedding dress. And the dinner for the guests prepared by the hired buffet.

In the early afternoon it rained a lot. But as the wedding hour approached, the sky opened and the wedding could be held outdoors. The bride's father took the bride to the altar and handed her over to the groom who received her with great happiness. And it was dad.

Edgard never took his eyes off Julia. It was like there was no one there, they were comfortable and kissed all the time.

- I want to explore with you what true love is, I want to give you my romantic and cozy home to create a happy life, he said, certain that there will be no life other than the one they had to love.

Julia cried all the time, emotionally, while declaring her love to Edgar, in response to what he said about her love.

- Let's give way to love to find the chemistry of love between us, she said, knowing that this was the chance for them to unite their souls in life and give their heart with their love to

Edgar.

The wedding ceremony ended and the bride and groom went to greet the guests.

In the evening, dinner was served. The Buffet served barbecue and caprese salad; white rice, chicken medallion; flank steak, sun meat, termite and rump, made on the grill. And for dessert, assorted sweets, milk pudding were served; and the wedding cake. Soft drinks, mineral water and wine were served for drinks.

The night was lively with live music. It was after midnight, when the party ended. And all the guests left, the groom remaining with the bride.

The next morning the party organizers came to clean up and clean up the dirt in the pool and barbecue areas. At 12:00 pm lunch was served. And at 4:00 pm all the guests for lunch were already gone.

- Anyway, alone. - Said Edgar.

CHAPTER 18 - Don't ignore passion, love, or sex.

- I didn't want you to see me just by my breasts and my ass, to realize that there is a rich inner world in me, said Julia. - When the man realizes that the woman has a soul, he will no longer ignore the woman's love for him.

- You, more than anyone, know that most men still see women as servants of sex to satisfy the desires of men. - Said Edgard - We both know that a woman's sexuality is not just a vagina, it has a whole apparatus that makes a woman a goddess - uterus, ovary, clitoris, vaginal canal ..., but it must be recognized that for the common man he does not know the scientific side that involves the woman's sexual apparatus.

- Unfortunately, the woman is seen as the man's sperm deposit. This will never change. It has been that way since the world is world. And it will be like this forever, she said.

- We will not go down to the details of the woman's sexuality, otherwise we will have conversation for the whole night. I would rather have sex with you than keep arguing and we will not exhaust the woman's theories of sexuality, said Edgar.

- As our honeymoon is starting, I will not insist on the discussion of sexuality today, because men today have sex just to satisfy their physiological needs, not because I consider sex to be love, affection and complicity between men and women. the woman, said Julia.

Edgar avoided hitting his wife, because he saw that the matter was taking a more heated turn. It was after 5 pm, and popular philosophy tells the man to avoid having an argument with the woman after noon.

Julia understood her husband's silence and was silent too. But he hoped, that she would return to that discussion in less time than he could imagine.

They were mature and knew that each person tried to love her way, more by contemplating the nude to eroticize the man's desire for the woman. Of course, that discussion was unnecessary, since he should have directed all the talk of sexuality into their intimacy for that wedding night.

Julia realized that Edgar was not comfortable with her. Then she said: - I hope you love me and I hold myself in the highest regard, do not think that I am too confident, because I can assure you that I am not. I know what I want, what I need. I just need you, like my beloved man, with whom I fell in love. I have a lot of affection, and I want to share all my love with you, she said, apologizing for having provoked the discussion about the woman's sexuality. - It was unreasonable, I admit.

My love, don't worry. - He said.

I looked like a stupid woman who wanted to show off, she said. - I'm very happy to have managed to hook you. Glad I managed to marry you, a man with whom we have mutual feelings.

You know that until the moment you said yes, that you agreed to marry me and the priest said, kiss the bride, I didn't believe I was going to marry a woman like you. I recognize that you are too much of a woman to me. - He said. - Truth be told, I didn't believe that I would get married one day, due to my old age. Mainly marrying a young, beautiful and hot woman like you.

After the fiasco of my marriage with Silverio, I did not believe that I would get married again. Imagine! Marry twice in the same year, with different men. It was luckier than judgment. - She said.

The two bursts out laughing.

- I will do my best to make our marriage work. I will give you all my love and affection. You will not regret having married me. - She said, holding Edgar's face and kissing him, for a long time.

- It should be written in the stars that I was going to marry you. Because the day I saw you, my heart fell in love with you. I couldn't take my eyes off you, he said.

"You meant to take your eyes off my ass," she said. - Good thing I have a big ass, otherwise I would have gone unnoticed by you.

- I don't know what I thought when I saw you. It was magical, I felt out of breath. I don't think I thought of anything at that time. I just loved your female figure. - He said. - I had just come out of mourning the death of my companion of 30 years of living together. I wanted to get out of that widowed state. I had envisioned a woman under 40 who was still of childbearing age. And God gave me you to start a new life.

- This is the sincerest statement I have ever heard in my life as a woman. Thank you for choosing me to be your life partner. I'm sure that God made me for you. - She said. - Are you ready to kiss me every day and want to make love to me for the next 200 years? I am ready to be your wife for the next 200 years.

- Yes, I am ready and I will be able to show you what passion and love are, in that order. Every day I will show that I am worthy of your attention and your love. I will strive every day to make you happy by my side. - He said, pulling the chair to be closer to her to kiss her.

That passion was positive. They were very tender for each other. Both were charismatic, kind and gentle. It seemed that they lived together in other times, so much so that they matched each other. He just needed to guess what she wanted from him. It was the same with her. They had a lot in common with each other. They were suitable for each other. Certainly, the angels there in heaven were rooting for that love to be eternal.

During the honeymoon week, they didn't leave the house. They were sunbathing and swimming in the new house that Edgar had remodeled to put that woman inside that house. They took advantage of the 43-degree heat to enjoy themselves in the pool. Edgard revealed himself to be a true chef and an excellent barbecue. Especially that he knew that story that a woman is conquered by the stomach; and vice versa, which is why the two studied recipes for delicious dishes every day on the internet to make, pleasing each other, as it should be.

As they were governed by law No. 8,112, eight consecutive days of marriage leave were granted, they took advantage of every second to love and be with each other without reservation.

Edgar and Julia sunbathed inside the couple's new mansion, as if it were a resort and they were on vacation. There could be no more suitable place for the two lovebirds.

Edgar loved to put cream on Julia's favorite body parts. And she didn't mind sitting in the sun all day and cooling off in the pool. It was just the two of them practicing their honeymoon romance. Each wanted to surprise the other better, giving passion, love and sex.

They felt potentially capable of showing that they were worthy of each other's attention and of making each other happy. Kisses were given with love. Each revealing himself as a potential kisser. None of them wanted to lose a minute of the other's attention, showing that love is made with love.